One More Tomorrow

Sam Vickery

For Nana Jean and for Grandad Bill.

Your love, support and memory live on in the

hearts of those you left behind.

The Gratitude Page

Thank you to everyone who has helped to bring this book to the world. I was blessed to have a wonderful team of beta readers for this book, each bringing something different to the table. Julianne Vanstone, JL Morse, Sue Clarke, Anne Ross, Kirsten Meiklejohn, Philippa Wilmot, Vikki Young, and Nicola Williams, thank you all for your feedback and support.

To my readers, the people who buy my work, and especially to those who have been waiting, emailing and asking for updates on the next book release, thank you so much for your support and encouragement. It means the world to me that there are people out there who are looking forward to another story from me. Your enthusiasm motivates me beyond all measure.

And to my family. My children. My husband. Thank you. Thank you for giving me the time to write. Thank you for being who you are and letting me be me. I love you guys.

Chapter One

I can't remember a time in my childhood when I ever dreamed of being a mother. Whilst my sisters were cooing over their Tiny Tears dolls, rocking their chubby plastic bodies and jamming magic milk bottles into their oddly triangular mouths, I was in the garden digging a hole to Australia, or climbing up the tall oak tree to launch my teddy from the topmost branches, testing out the latest parachute I'd invented out of a paper napkin and a tangled ball of my mother's wool. I was reading about how planets are formed, or making clay sculptures – which I was sure would make me a famous artist. I was busy, and curious and relentless in my thirst for knowledge. Babies did not interest me in the slightest.

Susie next door had one, a dribbly, demanding six month old brother called Davey – runny gravy, I called him behind her back – who I heard squealing and crying through the thin walls of our terraced house every morning before the sun was even up. I would roll over, huffing and grimacing, pulling my pillow hard over my ears as I tried to block out his piercing intrusions. Babies did not let people sleep, I'd deduced from these frequent unwelcome awakenings.

Susie was a typically proud big sister. She would grin indulgently as he knocked over her carefully constructed tower of bricks, not caring that he was rudely interrupting our game, dragging us out of our imagined world of pirates, magic and adventure to wave a chewed rusk in her face. I hated him.

As I lay in my huge, grown up sized bed now with the pre-dawn haze filtering through the sheer blue curtains, Lucas's warm strong back pressed up against my side as he slept, I wondered if that was why I was being punished. If I had brought on my own misery through some sort of wicked karma. My disdain, or at least my disinterest in babies had carried on right up until I turned twenty-eight. I'd managed to come through school, university, marry Lucas and get a job teaching anthropology – a subject I adored – without ever considering the possibility of motherhood. Lucas had been surprised at my certainty that children were not to be on the cards, but he was willing to box up that dream if it meant keeping me. Everything had been just as it should have been. Life was ticking by, following my carefully crafted plan. Everything was perfect. Until my twenty-eighth birthday.

There had been too much vodka for both of us. Laughter, fumbling in the dark, wrapped together in a tangle of limbs and lust. A torn condom that went unnoticed until it was too late. A shared glance of panic and bewilderment in the morning that followed. And then, though I held on to my sense of normal, my orderly, controlled reality, though I grasped onto it with all my might, there was nothing I could do to take back that night. In a few moments of reckless passion everything had changed.

Suddenly, those doors which had been bolted shut, the lock rusted and unmoving, had been burst open with an explosion that shattered them into tiny little splinters. We had done something that could not be undone, and all at once a whole new path lay before us, shining with possibility. And for no reason I could fathom, without reason or logic, I just knew, *I knew* that I had to follow it. As soon as I realised a heart beat other than my own was fluttering inside my womb, depending on me for its very existence, I knew. I was going to be a mother. I wanted it more intensely than I had ever wanted anything. I felt fierce and strong and primal. This was what I was meant to do, I knew it.

Except it wasn't.

Eleven weeks. Eleven precious, wonderful weeks. That's how long I managed to keep him alive. Don't ask me how, but I knew it was a boy. My son. Eleven weeks he grew and developed and changed me in ways that could never be erased. And then, in a wave of crippling cramps and clotted blood, he was gone. My son. My angel.

After he left me, I found I was no longer complete. I was not the person I had been before, I was something new, something empty and lost. I couldn't go back now that I had seen what could be. I couldn't forget how it had felt to be a mother, to be needed so deeply, to love so hard. I couldn't undo it.

Lucas stirred beside me and I glanced through tear fogged eyes at the small silver clock on the bedside cabinet. It had been my mother's and hers before that, and every time I looked at it I remembered with vivid clarity how it had felt to wake up in her big bed as a small child, her tanned arm slung loosely over my torso, the shining silver clock ticking quietly beside us.

She would wake groggy and grumpy, and I would have to cajole her into the day, convince her it really was morning time, though she would groan and refuse to open her eyes. "Just five more minutes, my darling. It's still dark," she would moan from under the covers. I would huff and sigh and fidget impatiently beside her as she ignored me, trying to get a few more precious moments of rest. Then, as if a switch had been flicked on, she would suddenly be ready, throwing the blankets to the ground and grabbing me tight, pulling me in for a hug and kissing me all over my face. I would squeal and try to get away, though really I loved it. She would jump out of bed singing at the top of her voice, her grumpiness forgotten and buried, at least until the next morning. The clock filled me with nostalgia and sadness, yet I refused to part with it. Painful though they were, the memories of my mother were all I had left. They were better than nothing at all.

Lucas stirred again. I wiped my swollen eyes

against the pillowcase, though I knew he would know right away that I'd been crying for hours. That my night had been filled with the endless pacing and wicked nightmares I was fast becoming used to. He always wanted to talk, to get me to tell him every little detail of what was upsetting me. To share the horror of the nightmares, the stories I told myself in the dark quiet hours. It was pointless. He knew that as well as I did, but he kept on trying, pushing, wanting to be there for me, to fix everything. But I couldn't be fixed. He knew that too.

Sometimes Lucas would wake in those dark, lonely hours, despite my tooth-marked fist, my swallowed, muffled sobs. When he found me in such a state, he would look at me with those big brown eyes glistening in the moonlight with tears he wouldn't shed, his mouth pursed in indecision and sadness. He would take me in his arms and hold me tight until I pretended to fall back to sleep. His comfort never helped. I didn't deserve it. I wanted to suffer alone. I didn't want to see the look of anguish in his eyes.

On this occasion though, I had managed to get a hold of myself before he woke. He would know I'd been crying again, of course. He could always tell. But I wouldn't flaunt it. I never did. Perhaps this morning we could pretend it hadn't happened. I didn't have it in me to talk about it again. At least not yet.

I felt the feather-light touch of his fingertips as they grazed their way through my hair, making their way down my spine. I shivered, instinctively leaning into the security of his warmth. "Good morning," he said, his throat raspy with the after effects of sleep as he nuzzled into my neck.

"Good morning yourself," I replied, my voice falsely bright as I turned to face my husband. He pursed his full lips into a scowl as he caught sight of my puffy eyes and blotchy cheeks, his thick, dark brows furrowing. Even so, I thought, he was still indisputably good looking. His cheekbones were defined and strong. His eyelashes thick, his eyes a pool of rich chocolate. And under the thin sheets, I could make out the defined muscles of his chest and shoulders.

He was a big man at six and a half feet tall. Being only five feet and two measly inches myself, I had always liked that about him. I used to love it when he wrapped me in those massive arms, and made me feel like nothing could hurt me. These days, though, even he couldn't protect me from my pain.

"Rox..." he began, his voice deep and serious. I shook my head.

"Don't, Lucas. Don't. Not today." He twisted his lips again and gave me a long, stern look. Indecision flickered in his eyes. He gave a quick nod and pulled me wordlessly into his chest. I felt myself tense against him as he kissed the top of my head and sighed. Fearing his kindness would only make me start sobbing all over again, I cleared my throat and pulled away, hopping out of bed without meeting his eyes. I could feel his stare burning into my back. I wrapped my cotton dressing gown around my shivering body, pulling my thick dark hair out from under the collar as I headed for the bathroom. "Don't forget, we've got my sisters coming over for lunch today," I told him over my shoulder.

"As if I would forget a visit from the Cormack family," Lucas said, smiling, though it didn't meet his eyes. I paused by the bedroom door, looking at a framed photograph on the wall of my family from last summer. It made me smile every time I saw it, though I never failed to notice the empty space where my mother should have been. My younger sisters, Isabel and Bonnie were identical twins, yet their personalities could not have been more different. Isabel was introverted, sweet, and bordering on genius. We'd expected her to become a physicist, a computer programmer, an entrepreneur, or something equally brilliant and fitting to her intelligence. Yet, she'd surprised us all by choosing to go into social work. She'd actually turned down several promotions because they meant moving away from the personal, one on one duties with the families and children she worked with, to go and push papers around an office instead. Isabel had explained that no pay rise in the world would be enough to pull her away from the people who needed her most. I suspected she thrived on the drama and excitement. Isabel was at her absolute best in a crisis. She was down to earth despite her brilliance, and barely a day went by without us seeing one another.

Bonnie had a polar opposite character to Isabel. Her personality was nothing short of extreme. She was loud, flakey and possibly the most honest person I had ever known. She would say whatever she thought, no matter the consequences. Lucas had once told her she had no filter, to which she'd told him filters were for shifty people and at least he knew what she really thought of him. Thankfully, I had been informed, she liked him. A couple of her exes had not got off nearly so lightly. Though she could be wild and unpredictable, Bonnie was also the most empathetic person I had ever known. She could see right through pretence, right to the source of the pain. A skill she used often, and which proved more than a little annoying when I was trying to pretend I was fine, thank you very much!

As sisters, and as friends we were as close as it gets. Our father had passed away from cancer when the twins were just two. I had been four. And then, we had lost our mother fourteen years later. Now it was just the three of us left from our little family, and the losses had created an unbreakable bond between us. I turned from the photograph, facing Lucas now, and gave him a genuine smile, not the false happy mask I had been pasting on all week. "I know you would never forget," I said. "Thank you." He nodded as he watched me pick up my wash-bag and walk into the bathroom. I could feel his pitying stare burning into my back.

Chapter Two

I had washed away all traces of my less than restful night, and was chopping carrots and parsnips into neat little sticks to roast, when Bonnie strolled through the back door, placing two bottles of red on the worktop. "Hey Sis," she said, coming up beside me, brushing a brief kiss across my cheek. "How are ya doing?

I turned and hugged my little sister warmly, smiling up at her. Despite the fact that Isabel and Bonnie were two years my junior, they both towered over me. I was what Lucas referred to as petite and buxom, though I thought of it as plain old short and round. The twins were a far more elegant five foot seven a piece and it gave them long slender legs I had always slightly envied. Their features were identical, delicate cheek bones, long wild ginger hair and pale green eyes. Very different to my own much darker looks.

My hair was thick, chocolaty and silky. Where they were athletic, I was hourglass. Where they were the image of my mother, I was clearly my father's daughter. I'd never had any issue telling them apart, but these days even a stranger would have no problem distinguishing between the two of them. Isabel's skin remained milky pale and unblemished, but Bonnie had transformed herself into a work of art. Her left arm was covered from wrist to shoulder in bright tattoos. Her back and right thigh were becoming increasingly adorned too. Flowers, butterflies and tiny pixies, sprites and swirls of colour, that on first glance looked stunningly beautiful. Yet if you glanced again, you would see something more. Hiding behind the pretty petals were demons with sharp teeth, beneath the wings of a butterfly you could just make out the hollow eyes of a woman's skull. There was death and blood hiding where you least expected to find it.

I often wondered if Bonnie realised quite how much her tattoos reflected who she was. The bright facade covering a pool of darkness, pain, suffering. It was hard to believe the designs had been unconscious.

Bonnie pulled back now, holding me by the

shoulders, looking intently into my own blue eyes. "Roxy... No," she whispered. "Again?"

I pulled out of her hold and turned back to the chopping board, picking up a handful of carrots, though I already had more than enough, attacking them with the peeler. I didn't know how my sister could always tell, but somehow, she just could. She saw through my smile instantly, my pain as obvious as a flaming beacon to her. She was the one person who I could never hide the truth from, and sometimes that annoyed me beyond all measure. I wanted to remain hidden in the shadows. I wanted to pretend, just this once that it hadn't happened. That I hadn't let everyone down again. I did not want to be comforted, to hear her words of sadness and sympathy.

I slammed a knife into the hard flesh of the carrot, beheading it viciously. "What are you talking about, Bonnie?" I said briskly. "I'm fine. Everything's fine." I swallowed thickly, trying hard not to cry.

She sighed and placed her hands firmly over mine on the chopping board, forcing me to stop my massacre, though I didn't want to. "Don't do that Sis, this is me. I know you, remember? You don't have to pretend."

I shook my head and yanked my hands free, startling her. I could feel the angry tears brimming to the surface, and blinked, determined not to let them fall. "I don't want to talk about it."

"Fine, don't talk," Bonnie conceded, stepping back. "But don't hold it inside, Roxy. Acknowledge it. Please. It's too much for you to cope with alone. I won't let you do that to yourself."

"You're a fine one to talk!" I accused, hearing the venom coating my words, wishing I could stop it. "When do you ever spill your guts, hey? When was the last time you opened up to me?"

Bonnie just shrugged, unapologetic. "If I have something I want to say, I'll say it."

"Well, the same goes for me too, so just back off, okay?"

Bonnie stared silently at me for a moment, and then gave a small nod of defeat. Breathing hard, I picked up a bottle of wine from the counter and opened it, pouring a generous glass for myself and another for Bonnie. Wordlessly, I handed it to her and then took a swig of my own. The alcohol travelled through my veins, warming, calming. I took a deep breath and looked back at Bonnie. She was watching me over the rim of her glass, waiting. Hoping, I thought. Hoping I would give in and spill my heart. Bonnie liked to fix things. She liked to focus on my pain, Isabel's pain, anyone else's pain as long as it wasn't her own. But I couldn't give her anything. I wouldn't do it. Not today.

"How was the gig last night?" I asked instead, noticing the false cheery tone that emerged from my lips. I was being shrill. Bonnie scowled and pulled out a stool from the breakfast bar, taking a deep gulp of her wine. Resigned to the wall I had put up, she gave in and answered the question.

"Not bad," she conceded. "The crowd was better than I'd expected and Lewis got over the tonsillitis in time to go on. We almost had to cancel. Wouldn't have been much of a show without a singer," she shrugged, still serious.

"Are they going to book you again?"

"Yeah, I think so. We got given a card from another guy too, he wants to book us for a festival. Not sure we're going to do it though."

"You should. You need to say yes to everything that comes your way. Keep your options open, get yourselves seen. That's how you make it, Bon-bon."

"I suppose."

"Don't you *want* the band to do well? Is there something else you'd rather do?"

"It's not that... I just. Oh, I don't know. It doesn't matter." She looked up at me and I could see that she was coming full circle back to my problems again. "Look, Rox, I know you're going through a tough time, but..."

"Bonnie – " I pleaded cutting her off. I brought my hands up to my eyes, anticipating tears already. She always knew how to set me off. "I just want to have a nice day with my family. I don't want it ruined."

"It won't be –"

The door banged open and we both looked round to see Lucas walking into the room, carrying a bag of ice. "Oh, hey Bonnie," he smiled. "Nipped out to get more of this," he said, holding up his frosty loot. "It's bloody stifling today. We'll eat on the patio I think."

Bonnie nodded. I caught her throw a cool glance

in Lucas's direction, their eyes meeting briefly in mutual understanding. My stomach clenched as I watched them. I jumped up and crossed the room, smiling brightly and kissing him, desperately trying to show them both that I was okay. "I'm going to set the table while we wait for Isabel," I announced brightly, picking up a tray stacked with glasses and cutlery and heading outside. Lucas watched me go, and I couldn't miss the deep frown furrowed into his brow.

I stepped out into the bright, July sunshine, but rather than setting the cutlery out ready for our lunch, I placed the tray quietly down on the bleached wooden table and stole around the side of the house, crouching beneath the kitchen window to listen in.

"It happened again, didn't it?" Bonnie was saying, a statement more than a question. Cautiously, I turned in a squat, leaning in against the wall. I raised myself up so I could peer through the window that looked in over the sink. The windowsill was covered in colourful ceramic pots, all containing fresh herbs that I had grown from seed. I peered beneath a bushel of overhanging coriander and saw my husband crouched beside the freezer, the drawer half open. He pushed it closed and remained unmoving, his shoulders slumped in defeat. Slowly, he stood up, slamming the freezer door and bracing himself against it. He spoke without turning to face Bonnie, his head lolling to rest against the door.

"She won't say. But yes. I'm sure of it. There was blood earlier this week. A lot of blood. But she won't talk."

Bonnie let out a whoosh of air, and squeezed her hands into fists. "Shit." She jumped off the stool and strode over to where Lucas was standing, placing her hand on his shoulder. I felt a sharp stab of guilt that she was comforting him when I should be, and for a second I contemplated going back inside.

Lucas turned slowly to face Bonnie and I saw the sadness in his eyes. His pain was my pain. And yet I was shutting him out completely. I knew I was being unfair to him, I knew I should talk to him about what was happening, but everything we could say had been said before. We had been through this same story too many times to have anything new to add to the pile, so I cut him off, my sadness too much for me to bear, unwilling to add his hurting to my burden. I was a horrible person and I knew it.

Bonnie scowled, her fists swinging restlessly at her sides, unsure where to direct her frustrations. And then, she grabbed the bear of a man, pulling him down into a tight hug. "Oh, Lucas, I'm sorry. I know this hurts you just as much as it hurts her. I'm so fucking sorry, it's not fair."

Lucas said nothing for a moment. "Me too," he finally rasped, pulling back and wiping at his eyes. *Was he crying?* I stared hard, trying to see better. My calves were beginning to burn, but I didn't dare to move in case they heard me. "I don't know what to do," he continued. "I don't know how to make it stop happening. This was the fifth time. Can you even believe that? The fifth fucking time. How is that fair? Why does it keep on happening?"

"I know," Bonnie shook her head. "Roxy doesn't deserve this. Neither do you."

"Nobody does," Lucas said wryly. "I can't keep putting her through this. There has to be a cut off point. It's killing her."

"You mean, you want to stop?"

"I want to protect her. From everything. There is

so much pain. Too much fucking pain. It's reckless to keep going."

I bit my lip hard, wanting to put my hands over my ears, but unable to stop myself from listening to more. He couldn't be about to say it, could he? He wouldn't do that to me, to us!

Bonnie's voice drifted out to me. "But it's what she wants. What you both want, isn't it?"

Lucas sighed and bowed his head. "I did. But maybe I'm not willing to pay the price anymore." He ran his hand roughly over his chin, and I noticed that he hadn't shaved. As I took a moment to appraise him, I realised how dark the circles around his eyes had become. How sunken his cheek bones. This was killing him too.

"There are other options we can pursue," Lucas continued wearily. "It doesn't have to be the end. But she won't even talk about it. I don't know what else I can do." My attention was suddenly drawn towards the road, the sound of a car pulling up. *Isabel.* Swiftly and silently, I moved away from the open window, and busied myself at the table as if I had been there all along. But I couldn't get Lucas's words out of my head. *Other options we can pursue.* How could he even think of stopping before we'd succeeded? How could he give up on us, on our family?

I wouldn't let him. I would never give up.

Chapter Three

The second time I miscarried was harder than the first. Lucas and I had sat long into the night after that first loss, cuddling in front of the open fire on the living room floor, mourning our baby and making the life changing decision that becoming parents was what we truly wanted now. We would try again and this time we would get to hold our baby. After all, miscarriage was remarkably common, and we'd had our share of the bad luck now. We would do it right this time.

We visited the doctor, we both took the vitamins. We ate well and both of us gave up drinking even refusing half a glass of wine. Lucas had said we were in it together. It wasn't fair that I had to give everything up if he wouldn't make the effort too. We planned and prepared and we felt sure that this time we would succeed.

Only we didn't.

I'd fallen pregnant that first month of trying. It was so easy. It felt right, the missing piece of the puzzle we hadn't known we were searching for. I had laughed that I didn't even have morning sickness, so sure that I was in for a smooth easy pregnancy after a rocky false start. We'd had an early scan at seven weeks just to be sure, crying together over that little flicker of a heartbeat enclosed within a tiny nugget of cells and information. Our baby. Alive and thriving. We had told everyone, celebrated joyously.

A few weeks later I'd been at work – right in the middle of teaching, when I'd been overcome with sudden, crippling cramps and had to abandon my students mid lecture. And then, just like that, it had been over. No more baby. Gone. Just like that.

After that second loss, fear had set in. This baby hadn't been some accident. Losing our child hadn't been just plain old bad luck. We couldn't call it a fluke any longer. Now, we had lost two of them. *I* had lost two of them, and we couldn't pass it off as an unlucky one off experience. It was so much harder than the first time. That little bean on the monitor had been our child. We had seen the life there and yet somehow, it was gone, just faded away out of reach and we could never get it back. It was heartbreaking.

The third time had been just five months later. I had known from the beginning that something wasn't right. My sisters had tried to reassure me, after all, who wouldn't be nervous in my position? But I'd felt off from the very start, and my instincts turned out to be right. That time had ended the worst. I had collapsed in the middle of the Saturday market, screaming in agony, crying out to the passing strangers to help me, sure I was dying. An ectopic pregnancy, the doctors had told me when I'd regained my senses after the emergency surgery. The embryo had attached to the inside of my right fallopian tube and as it grew too large, ruptured it completely. I had lost my third child and halved our chances of being able to conceive in one brutal swipe.

Bewildered as to why my body was betraying me, I had booked in to see the best fertility doctors in the country. I'd passively submitted to every test they had going, hoping beyond hope that they would find something fixable. Both Lucas and I had blood tests, genetics cross matching to determine whether the fault was down to gene compatibility. Nothing was found. I was a mystery. And I was broken.

By this point, I couldn't think about anything besides becoming a mother, birthing my child, holding that little sweet smelling, soft skinned bundle in my arms. I wanted it so much I could barely breathe, yet every time I had to deliver the news to Lucas, to my sisters that another baby was gone, my heart broke. As time passed, I had found myself hating my body. Wondering what I had done to deserve this pain over and over again.

The fourth time I had kept my mouth shut. I never told a soul that I was carrying another precious baby. When I'd been sick, I had hidden it. When I'd felt tired, I'd resisted napping, or if I was desperate, slipped into my office and locked the door, curling up beneath my desk for a few moments of respite. I'd become consumed with the idea that if I didn't tell anyone, my baby would survive. When the bleeding had started, I'd pretended it wasn't happening. When Lucas had confronted me, his eyes brimming with hurt tears, devastated that I was no longer confiding in him, I had denied it. I could not accept another miscarriage. I wouldn't take this any longer. I was going to have my baby. This baby. Only I wasn't. I couldn't. I'd fucked it all up again. My child was gone and no amount of refusal to admit it was going to bring him back to me.

The cracks began to deepen. Lucas and Bonnie had watched me closer, and the more they'd watched, the less I'd shared. I knew they knew. But to put words to what was happening was too much for me to bear. In the beginning, we had cried together. Comforted each other, supported one another. But now, I knew that this was something that only I could fix. I was the one who wasn't strong enough to protect our babies. I was the one who kept fucking this up for everyone. I couldn't lean on them because they could never understand it was my fault. They wouldn't accept what I knew – that I was a failure. I had promised myself that I wouldn't ever open my heart to them again. Not until I'd conquered this challenge.

By the fifth miscarriage, the one I'd had just a few days ago, I was almost numb. I had lost hope. I no longer believed I could carry a child to term, though it was all I wanted in the world. Now I just waited for the cramps to begin, the bleeding to show. I couldn't give up, I couldn't see a life where I could be content without my baby, yet I could feel my body losing strength. The insomnia was frightful. I would pace the darkness of our home for hours every night, tears flowing uncontrollably. If Lucas tried to comfort me, I pushed him away. If Isabel or Bonnie tried to talk about it, I would shut down completely. I was losing myself, I could feel it. But I didn't know what to do about it. I was running through a nightmare, my baby being swiped from my arms, the demons stealing him from his bed, and I would chase them to the ends of the earth. But I could never seem to catch them.

Chapter Four

Oxford, in the mornings before the hustle and bustle of the tourists mingling about, the mums and kids on the school run and the students cluttering up the streets, was – in my opinion – the most peaceful place in the world. I loved to walk along the river as the sun was coming up, taking a meandering stroll down to the university where I worked as a professor. It struck me as amusing to realise quite how much I enjoyed seeing those first rays of sun smile weakly down on the world.

I hadn't always been an early bird, in fact, the friends I'd had during my time as a student in the very same uni would've been amazed if they had caught even a glimpse of me before brunch. I'd always liked the quiet of the night, the surreal element to walking home under the soft glow of moonlight. There was something special about night-time, and back then, I had been at my most productive in the wee hours. Assignments were written at three a.m, projects planned and executed under the dim lamp at my little scratched desk while the world slept around me. I would fall into a deep, restful sleep in the early hours, raising my head as the church bell chimed midday.

These days, not so much. It wasn't that I'd traded being a night owl for the role of early bird. More that I couldn't sleep no matter what time it was. I still saw three a.m most nights, but it wasn't in a frenzy of productivity. More a desperate exhaustion accompanied by a spinning mind I couldn't seem to quiet. If I slept at all, it was short, light and restless and I had become more than just acquaintances with dawn since the baby saga began.

However, to my continued surprise, there had been little silver linings to the early starts. Walking in the pure, new light, noticing tiny, wonderful things like the glimmering drops of dew on the grass, the smell of fresh crisp air undisturbed by traffic fumes and cigarettes and stale perfume. The birds singing their morning chorus. It all helped. It made me feel small in the universe. Made my problems insignificant in the great scheme of things, if only for a moment. I could forget, just for a little while. I could feel at peace.

I'd spent the weekend fretting that Lucas would try to talk to me, to tell me he wanted to stop trying for a baby, but to my immense relief he hadn't broached the subject. Now, as Monday morning dawned, already hot and bright, I hoped that he'd been speaking in haste. Bonnie had caught him at a bad time, he'd been understandably sad, grieving another loss I had refused to include him in. It was no wonder he'd had a moment of doubt about pushing forward, carrying on. I didn't believe he would insist we stopped. Not when he knew how much it meant. To both of us.

As I approached the university, one of the first to be milling around so early in the day, I felt myself break into a smile. It would all be okay. It had to be. The old, beautiful building always made me feel calmer, and I loved stepping onto the grounds, wondering what the day held in store for me. I had never intended to teach, never intended to end up in this same old building where I'd discovered my passion for anthropology all those years back. Where I had met and fallen in love with Lucas. But, I reflected, life had a way of sending us in directions we never expected to go. For me, my dream had been to travel. To live amongst the tribes I'd researched. To be a real, intrepid, cultural anthropologist. I had wanted to completely submerge myself in another world, another culture, to watch how the people interacted, how they raised their children, see who they answered to, what they valued. I had wanted to know them on a deep level, to know what they cared about, not just read about it all on a piece of lifeless paper.

I could still pull up that memory of my very first field trip not long after I had started at uni. The smell of the hot, dusty earth. The musical tones of a foreign tongue. The feeling of absolute rightness that this was what I was meant to do. This was my path. Tanzania had changed everything for me. But it wasn't to be. My mother had been too unwell for me to continue travelling so far afield. And then, she was gone, and it didn't seem right to walk away and leave my siblings to pick up the pieces. So I had shelved that aspiration. Put it in a box and created a new one. And though it had never been my first choice, I had come to realise it wasn't second best.

I had found I enjoyed talking about anthropology just as much as I enjoyed being amongst the tribes people. It was utterly stimulating and I was fulfilled in my work. I loved my students, fed off their energy, their passion and zest. It was affirming to connect with other people, young, unjaded minds who loved the topic as much as I did. So in the end, giving up the dream to travel didn't feel like too great a sacrifice to bear. I had moved forward, making the choice to revel in my students and their success. I would adapt. And after that first brush with pregnancy, the plan had shifted to include motherhood. Something that would be far more suited to the life of a professor than an explorer. The two went together in my mind so beautifully, I had known it was right. It was what I was meant for. It was a good dream. But so far, a huge chunk of the puzzle had not slotted into place.

As I left the already sultry air of the outside world and let myself into my office, my phone rang softly in my bag. *Lucas,* I thought before I had even glanced at the display. He would be waking up now, wondering where I was, why I had hurried off to work so soon. Again. He knew I was avoiding him. I could see the pain in his eyes every time I looked his way.

For a second, I considered cancelling the call, but then my thumb was swiping across the screen and I was lifting it to my ear. I wanted to hear his deep soothing tones. I wanted to tell him to please stop worrying, it would be okay, I would make it better... Somehow.

"Morning sweetie," I said, plopping my bag down on my desk and sinking into my squashy leather chair. I loved this chair, it made me feel so much more grown up than I knew I really was. It looked like a chair someone who had their shit together would own. A professional's chair.

"Where are you?" came his croaky voice. He'd obviously not had coffee yet.

"At work. Lots to do today."

"At this time? Couldn't you sleep?"

"Do I ever?" I joked, my tone light, trying to keep him away from the serious stuff. "What about you, got a busy day ahead?"

"Think so... I seem to remember Sue telling me that Mrs. Rodriguez is coming in with Snickers again."

"Oh no!" I laughed. Sue was Lucas's receptionist, and Snickers was a cantankerous old cat with a special hatred for the vet. Unfortunately for Lucas, he held that title. After his last appointment to remove a deeply embedded thorn from between the pads of Snickers' toes, Lucas had come away with four deep claw marks down the inside of his arm, and a bite mark on his hand which had taken two weeks to heal. Lucas never seemed to lose his sense of humour with the animals though. He was unendingly patient, and always forgave them, even crotchety old Snickers.

"Did I tell you about the box of baby hedgehogs we had in yesterday?" he laughed, as if on cue.

"No, tell me," I smiled, picturing his rumpled bed hair as he spoke.

"Those little creatures are faster than they look — and did you know they can climb? We had a challenge keeping track of them all!"

I laughed, picturing the scene. Though a big, intimidating man to look at, Lucas was surprisingly soft and tender when it came to animals. He often had an amusing story about a rabbit on the loose or a cat with an attitude to regale me with. I'd noticed, though I never mentioned it, that he kept the sadder stories to himself. He must have to do some horrible things as a vet. Say goodbye, and watch as people lost their beloved pets. Make some tough decisions. Fight battles that couldn't be won. But Lucas never shared any of that side of his work with me. I knew he was protecting me, sure that I couldn't handle any more tears in my week, and I was grateful. I was also racked with even more guilt at not supporting him emotionally, as a wife should.

"Anyway, Rox..." he said suddenly, his voice no longer cheery, but firm and serious now. "Tonight... we, ah... we need to sit down. To talk."

A lump wedged itself in my throat as my fingers clenched tightly to the phone. "About what?" I whispered.

"Let's just wait till tonight, yeah? Come straight home. Okay, Roxy?" I could hear the nerves in his voice. He meant it. We would be talking, whether I wanted to or not. I wasn't ready. What if he said the worst? That he wanted to stop trying? Or even that he didn't want to be with me anymore? That he couldn't stand my failings? No, Lucas wouldn't say that. He wouldn't want to hurt me. But...what if? My mind spun with all the dreadful possibilities. Why did he have to call now to tell me? Why not wait until I got home, spring it on me then? Now I had to endure a full day of fear, not knowing what he was going to say. I could feel the tears stinging my eyes and I knew I had to get off the phone before I fell apart. I *couldn't* fall apart, it wasn't fair.

"Okay," I managed to choke out. "I have to go." I cut off the phone and stared into nothingness, numb with fear, heavy tears already weaving silent streams through my make-up.

Chapter Five

My walk home was far less enthusiastic than the walk into work had been. I'd been dreading it all day, ever since Lucas had told me he wanted to talk. At lunch I'd taken two bites of my sandwich, only to be overcome with crippling stomach cramps, the nerves churning my insides into a knotted mess. I'd barely made it to the bathroom in time to bring the entire contents of my stomach up, my head lolling mournfully over the bleach stained toilet bowl.

At the sinks as I'd rinsed out the bile from my mouth, one of my colleagues had made a joke about morning sickness. For a brief moment I'd considered slamming my fist into the bitch's mouth. Making her realise how deep her words had cut. Instead, I had laughed hollowly and made a speedy exit. Probably for the best, I'd reflected after the wave of fury had died down. Not worth getting fired over some insensitive small talk.

The more I thought about the looming discussion with Lucas, the more I was sure he would tell me something I couldn't bear to hear. That our time to try for a baby was up, that he couldn't do it anymore. The thought sent tremors of cold fear through me. I needed him. I needed his understanding, his support, his fucking sperm! How would we ever be able to move forward from here without achieving our longed for goal of having our baby? Our own child. How could the relationship survive with just the two of us?

On a whim, I crossed the road, heading for Isabel's place rather than my own home. Delaying the inevitable. I loved that my sister lived so close to me. I could actually see the entrance to my cul-de-sac from her living room window. It was comforting to have her so near, so that I could pop in for a quick chat, or lose myself for a while when I couldn't face going home. Like now.

I tapped lightly on the freshly painted blue door, and heard the click-clack of her heels approaching. I smiled. Isabel lived in stilettos, a fact that bemused and baffled me considering she was far from short. She said they made her feel ready for anything which seemed an odd statement to me, considering I could barely cross the room in such towering footwear without falling on my face.

"Rox!" she grinned as the door swung open. She kissed me on the cheek and stepped back so I could enter. "How are you?"

I shrugged. "Not bad," I answered, though it was far from the truth. "Thought I'd stop in for a cuppa on my way home."

Isabel nodded. "It's lovely to see you. Bonnie's here too. In fact..." she paused, as I hung my cardigan over the bannister, "she's moved in." She nodded towards the open door of the living room and my eyes followed her gaze to a pile of bin bags stuffed full, presumably with Bonnie's belongings.

"Moved in? Why?"

"She was evicted. She's not saying much about it though."

"Fuck. I asked her if she needed a loan last month and she flat out refused me."

"Me too. I don't think it was about the money though," Isabel said, carefully lowering her voice. "I think it's more to do with the parties. There have been... complaints."

"It's that bloody band. They act like a bunch of hormonal teenagers," I shook my head.

"Maybe," Isabel said. Her eyes didn't quite meet mine, and I suddenly got the impression she knew more than she was saying. Isabel was very good at keeping secrets. Like the time she'd had a boyfriend for six months and we didn't find out until after she ended it. Or the time she took driving lessons and didn't tell a soul until after she passed her test. Or, I thought wryly, the time she knew that mum was flushing her pills down the toilet, but had begged Isabel not to tell the rest of us. That one she'd kept to herself for a long time. By the time she'd told us, it was already too late. I shook my head, clearing away the thought. This was not the time for that discussion. It wasn't like we hadn't been over it a thousand times before anyway. It was a topic we avoided at all costs these days.

"Anyway," Isabel continued, "She's in the kitchen. You can ask her yourself. Come on, I'll put the kettle on." I followed her through to the bright sunny kitchen where Bonnie was sat at the breakfast bar, picking pieces off a chocolate muffin and popping them into her mouth. Her lips were painted a glossy red and the contrast to her fiery hair had a dramatic effect. She smiled as I entered the room.

"Thought it might be you, Rox. Come to avoid the husband then?" she grinned. God she knew how to touch on a raw nerve. I felt something snap inside me as I took a step towards her.

"Bonnie, did you say something to Lucas on Saturday? About me? About... about us having a baby?" I asked, knowing the answer already.

"About the fact that you're prepared to kill yourself for something that might never happen?" she replied, her tone almost cold. I was unprepared for how hurtful the impact of her words would be. I felt suddenly breathless and dizzy, like I'd been punched in the stomach. I took a step back and leaned against the kitchen door to steady myself.

"Bonnie, it's not your place... You have no idea... People lose babies and then go on to have healthy pregnancies, it's just n–not happened for us yet – "

"Roxy."

Tears sprang to my eyes as she stared at me and I wiped at them angrily. I didn't want to cry. I needed to show them, to show Lucas how strong I was. I could do this. I *did* have it in me. Of course I didn't need to give up. Isabel flicked the switch on the kettle and walked towards me. She handed me a tissue and put her arm around my shoulder. "Bonnie wasn't gossiping about you for fun, Rox. She was worried. Lucas is worried. *I'm* worried. We don't want to lose you." She squeezed my shoulder tightly. "I saw him on the way into work this morning. He looked dreadful. He said you won't talk to him. Why won't you talk about this?" she asked, her forehead creasing in worry. "We're here for you, Rox, all of us. You need to lean on us."

I put my hand to my head feeling a knot of tension building in my temples. "I can't."

Bonnie slammed her coffee on the kitchen side, the noise startling me. "This is ridiculous! You can't keep this up, Roxy. It's going to destroy you! Lucas said – "

"No, Bonnie! No!" I cried, rounding on her with fury. "I don't want you talking to my husband about this. It's between me and him. It's our business, not yours!"

"And what does he think? Hmm? Do you even know? Have you even asked him?" she shouted, her eyes flashing with fury. "Have you even considered that he might like a say in the matter?" She stood, gripping the edge of the counter, composing herself. After a long, uncomfortable silence, she looked up at me. "I'm sorry. I shouldn't have shouted. I'm sorry, Rox. But I'm just so worried about you. I can't understand why you keep putting yourself through it, over and over again. It's like picking a scab. Isn't it time to let it heal?"

She walked across the kitchen and stopped in front of me. "Roxy..." she said softly. She wiped a tear away from beneath my eye with the pad of her thumb. "I love you. I know what this means to you, of course I do. But how long can you keep putting yourself through it? Five miscarriages in a row... it's affecting your health sweetie. We can all see the change in you, not just the sadness but everything."

Isabel nodded in agreement as she handed me another tissue. She chewed at her bottom lip, her pale eyes filled with concern. "Bonnie's right sweetie. You're losing so much weight, you're so pale, and I know you hardly sleep. Lucas told me he wakes up most nights to find you gone from the bed. You can't keep pushing forward recklessly. You need to think of your health, your marriage."

Anger surged through my veins. I pushed away from them, sneering. "What about my marriage? You both know so much about what's going on with my life do you? Is that what he wants to talk to me about tonight, huh? That he's sick of me? Wants to stop or he's going to leave, is that it? How nice for you all to spend so much time discussing my private matters without me. Aren't I lucky to have you three making choices on my behalf!"

"If you confided in your husband once in a while, maybe asked what he thought of the situation, perhaps he wouldn't need to share his concerns with us!" Bonnie bellowed, throwing her hands up in the air in exasperation. She took a step back and breathed deeply, squeezing her fingers over her mouth as if she could hold back her words. Her nails were painted the same pillar box red as her lips and despite my fury, I thought she looked like something out of a painting in her despair.

Isabel was balling a tissue between nervous fingers, breaking off little pieces and dropping them at her feet. She hated confrontation. "Look, Roxy," she said, her voice tentative and gentle. "We just want what's best for you. I know you want a baby, but there are other ways to make a family that aren't going to kill you. Please, just think it through okay? We don't want to lose you too."

I felt the guilt flooding through me as the words left my sister's mouth. I knew how scared she was. How devastated they'd been by our mother's illness and subsequent death. Our mother, Rosie, had suffered with severe Bipolar disorder throughout the whole of my teen years. I still don't know why or how it came on, but once it hit, there was no turning back for our family. She had been a storybook mother for the first twelve years of my life, before suddenly transforming into a complete stranger, seemingly overnight.

At first, it had been almost fun to have such a cool parent. I could still remember being woken by my mum long after midnight, pulled from my bed and dressed in a sequin jumpsuit before being led into our small back garden. I was twelve years old. Isabel had been guarded and confused as Rosie had insisted she get up and put on her best party dress, but mum had soon convinced her to lighten up and enjoy the festivities. Bonnie had needed no encouragement, she hadn't stopped squealing in utter delight. We'd lit the floodlights, turned the music up loud and had our first taste of alcohol as our mother had made sickly sweet, ridiculously strong cocktails for all of us.

I can still remember the laughter. We'd been creased double, our sides aching, breathless with mirth. We'd jumped on the trampoline, holding hands to steady each other, tipsy and stumbling and then laughing all over again. Bonnie had said that mum had begun crying over something at one point, but I couldn't picture it now. We'd been told later, though none of us had any recollection of it, that the police had been called by several of our neighbours. Our Auntie June, Mum's sister had been called, finding the twins vomiting and mum in a terrible state, bellowing like a banshee and throwing handfuls of lettuce at anyone who approached her. (I remember finding this utterly hilarious every time it was brought up in the years to come).

I, apparently, had fallen asleep on the kitchen floor, and had to be carried upstairs by a policeman. I had no memory of this either. Auntie June had told us dribs and drabs of the story, mainly in the midst of a row with my mother, which became an ever frequent occurrence as Rosie's condition deteriorated. She would spit little titbits out, accusing and bitter, until we had collected all the pieces of information, figuring out what had occurred that night. I could never be sure her version was the entire story though. My mother had no memory of what we had done either, so couldn't say otherwise. That night could have ended so badly for all of us, but after reasoning at length with the police, Auntie June had somehow convinced them to let Rosie go with just a caution. These days I'm not sure we would have been so lucky.

It was a memory the twins and I both treasured and hated in equal measures. It had been a crazy, unpredictable adventure, something so unorthodox we couldn't help but enjoy ourselves, yet it had also been the first night we had all realised something was a little off with our mother, though it would be a long time until we understood quite how bad things were for her. The years that had followed had been hard. Mum had brought home a stream of men, partying hard, and fighting harder. She would go out to clubs and start a brawl with anyone who dared to look at her the wrong way. She was always sporting bruises, either on her knuckles, her face or both.

She'd been admitted into a mental hospital on three separate occasions, each stay spanning months. Our now deceased, and very beloved grandparents had come to live at our house to take care of us, and it had felt once again like a party, all be it with an uneasy undertone to it. Mum had always come out of hospital calm, serene, ready to be there for us, to make it all up to her family somehow. But each time, she had slipped back down into the mania again. Or worse, the dark, desolate depression that never seemed to end.

Rosie had hated taking the pills, insisted that she didn't need medicine, that she was all better. She never could see that it was the pills that were the reason for her sanity. That they were the only reason she wasn't streaking naked through the streets or sobbing in the shower with a blade to her wrists.

As I got older and my grandmother explained her condition to me, I began to see it for myself. I saw how she relied on the medicine to keep her sane. The differences that crept in as the days passed without it. I would beg her to swallow the pills. I would crush them and mix them in her tea, so desperate was I to keep her safe. It rarely worked. She would pretend. She would lie. She would swear she had taken them already. And when she was discovered, she would plead with whoever had found her to keep her secret. Even knowing what would happen, Isabel hadn't been able to betray her. I knew she blamed herself for what happened in the end.

My mother, my real mother, the one before the mental illness, the mother who liked to lie in and who could play pirates as good as any child, the woman who would patiently sit with a net, waiting to catch the brightest butterfly in the garden just so we could have the pleasure of setting it free again, would have never dreamed of lying to me. My mother who had brushed and plaited my hair each night before bed, couldn't possibly be the same woman who had slapped me hard across the face for trying to convince her to take a little blue tablet. I spent most of my teen years trying to get her back. The mother I had grown up with. I didn't want this person, this imposter. It was as if a demon from another world had crept inside her and taken over her mind. And I was terrified.

I didn't want a mother who allowed me to throw as many parties as I liked. I didn't want her to offer me alcohol and cigarettes, and one time, cocaine. I didn't want any of it. I just wanted *my* mum back. The real version of her. It was a wish that had never come to pass.

When it came to the end, it had been me who had found her. Me who'd been the one to have to call the police. It seemed fitting. After all, it had been me who'd resisted this new version of her so vehemently. I had wanted her gone. But I hadn't wanted this. Not ever. I hadn't even bothered to call an ambulance. The body was a shell, cold and hard, life long since departed. The corpse was swinging from the frayed brown rope we had kept for emergencies in the shed. I'd noticed every little detail. I wish that I hadn't.

Those intricate images haunted my dreams for years. The colour of her toenails, translucent pink against pale stony feet. The knife on the table, clean of blood. The smell of burning beef and tomatoes. She had left a stew, of all things bubbling dry on the stove, a note beside it. It had read,

I thought it would be easier if I cooked before I left.

That was all. No declaration of love. No apology, no sadness. I don't know if it made it better or worse that she was clearly out of her mind insane at the point of her suicide. Would it have been easier if she'd thought it all through and still gone ahead with it? I doubted it.

Though I had been the one to find her body, it had been Bonnie and Isabel who had taken it the hardest. They were still so young, just sixteen years old, and they had already had so much loss to cope with. And though I hadn't realised it at the time,

Isabel was drowning in guilt. When Rosie had abandoned them, *us,* without so much as a goodbye, something in them changed. Bonnie had gone from fun loving, to completely wild. She had disappeared off for months at a time, abandoning all thoughts of college, instead partying and drinking and cutting herself off from the chance of ever being hurt again. Isabel had put her head down and lost herself in her studies, filling any spare second of free-time with volunteer work. She had pasted on a smile and forged ahead, but I knew there was a deep fear within her. She was terrified of losing anyone else and she held on tight to the few that she had left. Bonnie. And me.

And now, here I was risking myself for a child I may never get to hold. I was threatening her safe little bubble with my actions, and I knew I was hurting her deeply. But I couldn't walk away from my dream just to protect them, could I? I couldn't just stop.

I reached out to place my hand on Isabel's folded arms. "You won't lose me, sweetie. I promise. I'm stronger than I look," I insisted, my eyes on her pale, freckled face. I could see she was holding back an ocean of pain just beneath the surface. "Don't you see, I have to keep trying. But you won't lose me," I repeated, my gaze moving to Bonnie now, my tone pleading, inviting them both to give me their blessing.

Bonnie looked at me, her eyes shining with angry tears. She shook her head. "You don't know that." Then she turned and stormed out of the house, slamming the door behind her. My hands shook as I watched her go.

Chapter Six

I couldn't stop pacing as I waited for Lucas to arrive home. He'd sent a text an hour before saying that he was sorry but he'd been held up, though of course he didn't tell me with what. Probably some horrible emergency with a poor, injured animal. Perhaps right now he was working tirelessly to save someone's beloved pet. My stomach churned at the thought of it. As per usual, I would just have to wonder though. I knew I would never find out, Lucas wouldn't be sharing his burdens with me. That was a habit that needed to change, I realised now as I wiped the duster over the dining room table for the third time in a row.

I was wearing pretty black shoes with a low heel, and a green mini dress that I knew Lucas loved on me. I had already showered, put on make-up and had a big pan of pork and apple stew bubbling away on the stove. I was going into battle and I knew it. I would attack him with intense kindness, show him the bright, light-hearted, productive side of myself – my best side. I would make him realise that I was not the frail, failure of a woman I was certain he had begun to see when he looked at me. No longer would he come home to find me curled up in a ball on the sofa, dressed in old grey pyjamas. He wouldn't get the usual monotone one word answers to his questions. Not anymore. I was going to win him over with love. I had to get him on my side, I had to make things better for him.

As I dropped the duster into the washing machine and stirred the stew again, I realised how unfair I had been on my husband. Bonnie and Isabel were right, it wasn't okay for me to shut him out like this. It wasn't fair to him that he couldn't talk about the things that upset him with the one person who should always be there for him. He couldn't share his sadness over his working day. And he hadn't been able to discuss the pain he felt over our lost babies in a very long time. I had cut him off, walked away, refused to hear the words that cut me to the bone.

Yet my efforts to protect myself from the sickening pain I felt over my lack of a baby, had caused him to feel shut out in the cold. Abandoned. I could see now that I was hurting him, and as much as I hated to admit it, Isabel *had* been right. I was hurting my marriage too. The love, the inseparable bond and unquestioning connection we had shared at the beginning, had been lost in recent years. There was a mountain between us that couldn't be scaled.

The time had come for me to play my part. To make some serious compromises. I would have to face the pain and open myself to him. I would have to drag myself out of the miserable bubble I had retreated into. I would smile and cook his favourite foods. I would make an effort with my looks and remind him that I was still here, I was still the woman he loved.

But I wouldn't agree to stop trying. I wouldn't give up that dream. No. I would convince him to continue. I would give him myself again, but I wouldn't stop trying for my baby. Not ever.

The key turning in the door made me jump, my elbow knocking against my mug of tea, almost sending it over the side of the kitchen counter. I grabbed it, righting it just in time, as Lucas walked into the room. I could see the dark circles under his eyes, the lines etched deeply into his furrowed brow. I wondered how they had become so deep without me noticing. I wondered if my own face showed the same marks of weariness.

I stood and walked towards Lucas, kissing him on the mouth and wrapping him in a silent hug. He instantly melted into me, his arms enveloping me within them, stunned into silence. The move was so familiar, so natural, yet I realised with a pang that I couldn't remember the last time I had approached him with affection. Sex yes, but no vulnerable hugs. No sweet kisses. I really *had* abandoned him. As I squeezed my eyes shut against his big, warm chest, I could feel the tension leave his body in increments.

"What's all this?" he asked finally, leaning back to appraise me. "You look lovely."

"Thank you. Dinner's ready, did you want it now or do you want to shower first?"

A flash of uncertainty passed over his face as he tried to work out what I was up to. "Uh, now I think. I missed lunch – I'm starving."

I nodded and moved towards the stove, taking two

deep bowls and ladling generous helpings of the steaming stew into them. My hands shook as I placed his in front of him.

"This looks great, Rox, thank you," he said, taking a wedge of bread from the board as I placed it in front of him. I pulled a chair out on the opposite side of the table and lifted a spoonful of the fragrant pork to my lips. The meat was cooked to perfection, but I found my mouth was as dry as a handful of sand, my tongue plastered to the roof of my mouth. I could barely manage to choke the mouthful down. Discreetly, I placed my spoon back on the table, instead picking up my wine glass and drinking deeply.

I had planned to wait, to let him eat and relax, to show him how well I was doing before approaching the sensitive topics. It was the clever thing to do. I had to be patient, act at the right time, not rush him into it. As I watched him eat, I felt as though I would explode if we didn't break into the tough conversation soon. I needed to resolve it, quickly.

Instead of diving in with the baby talk though, I reached forward and took his hand. "You were late back, did something happen at work?" I asked softly.

He shook his head, continuing to eat. He didn't look up as he answered through a mouthful of stew. "Nothing to worry about, just a glitch."

I watched him closely, sad at how little he wanted to share. "Lucas," I said sternly. He looked up at me and our eyes met. "Tell me what happened. Please? I want to know."

He held my gaze. "It was nothing."

I frowned and pursed my lips stubbornly. "Tell me."

He sighed and put down his spoon, wiping his mouth on the back of his hand. "Why? Why are you suddenly so interested in what happens at work? You don't usually care to ask. What's going on, Roxy?"

I played nervously with the stem of my wine glass, feeling my face burning with embarrassment. "I know. I..." I shook my head and took another sip of wine to steady myself. "Lucas, I am interested, I do want to know... I should know, I mean you have a whole other life I'm not a part of. I – I want to be," I sighed, looking up at him. "I want to be there for you. Even when it's horrible... I mean, especially when it is. You should have someone to talk about this stuff with."

He scowled and leaned back in his chair, regarding me coolly. I wasn't used to him looking at me this way, even when he was angry, he had always looked at me softly, his eyes always loving, warm. Not now. "It's been a bloody long time since I have been able to do that, Rox. Why start now?"

I swallowed thickly, determined not to cry. *Be strong, show him you're strong, don't fucking cry!* "I know," I conceded. "It's going to change, I promise, it's all going to change. I want us to be how we used to be. I want to hear what's happening... what you're feeling." I pushed back my chair and walked around the table to where he sat. Hesitating only for a second, I moved so that I was sitting in his lap, my fingers twirling through the back of his hair, just like old times. "I'm so sorry, Lucas, I'm sorry for shutting you out. I'm sorry I keep fucking it all up for us."

He sucked in a breath and I was shocked to see an expression of absolute fury cloud over his features. With a grunt, he heaved me from his lap and stood, striding across the kitchen, his huge fists clenched tightly. "Can you even hear yourself, Rox? Can't you see what a fucking mess this has all become, this whole baby situation? Can't you see what it's doing to you?"

One hand flew to my mouth as the other grasped the table for support. So we were here already, at the crux of it all. I wasn't ready, I couldn't do it. I gave a start as Lucas slammed his bear like fist down onto the counter. I had never in all our years together seen him like this.

"Lucas," I moved a step towards him, my hand outstretched. "Darling, please, calm down. There's no need to be so angry. Please, sit down."

He shook his head, looking at me as if I were raving mad, and for a second, I wondered whether I was. It did run in the family after all. "No need to be angry?" he growled. "Are you joking, Roxy? Do you think you married a complete fool, is that it? You think you can put on a pretty dress and cook me dinner and get your way?" He leaned over the counter towards me. "Do you think I *want* you to hate yourself, blame yourself for the miscarriages? How the fuck do you think that makes me feel, to know that my wife, the woman I love is destroying herself physically and emotionally, over and over again, all for something that might never happen?" he shouted.

I blushed to the roots of my hair, horrified at how easily he had seen through my actions. "Lucas, of course I don't think you're a fool. I just wanted it to be like old times, you know? J–just have fun with you, show you that I'm still, well, me." I balled my fists nervously at my sides, before rubbing one absently against the smooth wooden surface of the table in wide circles. "I just wanted to show you that I'm sorry," I gulped, blinking back the bastard tears that wouldn't relent. "I know..." I continued, my voice strangled with emotion, "I know that I haven't been fair to you. To anyone. I know that. It's been hard. Talking about everything, living the same nightmare over and over again." A sob broke free and I sank into the chair my husband had vacated, my hands covering my face. "I am so sorry. I know you're suffering too. I'm sorry it's not been smooth," I choked, wiping my nose on my sleeve.

Lucas gave a sigh and watched me for a moment, his expression softening. He walked around the kitchen counter and came to crouch down in front of me. "Look at me, Rox," he whispered softly. Slowly, I lifted my mascara smudged eyes to meet his. I was relieved to see the warmth in his expression. "We can't keep putting ourselves through this, my love. I know, believe me, I do know what having a baby means to you. I wanted it too, so very much." He stroked a strand of hair back from my face, tucking it behind my ear. "But this can't go on. It's killing you. And, honestly, it's killing me too. I won't keep doing this to us. I just won't, Roxy. It will destroy us both."

I shook my head frantically. "Lucas, please, don't say that." I reached out and grabbed him tightly by the shoulders. "Please don't give up on our family, I promise, things will be better. I won't shut you out, we will face whatever happens together. Just please, don't give up on our baby," I begged.

He shook his head, his eyes filled with pain. "No, Roxy. No. I'm sorry but we're done. I won't go through that again."

"No! You don't get to decide that. No!"

He made to stand up and I found myself moving before I even registered what was happening. I launched myself at him, kissing him roughly on the mouth, startling him so he fell back onto the tile. "Roxanne!" he gasped. "What the hell..." he managed to splutter, as I continued to kiss him desperately. My hands worked frantically at his belt, determined that I could make him change his mind. I *had* to make him change his mind.

Suddenly I felt myself grabbed hard around the arms and rolled ungracefully onto my back on the cold, hard kitchen floor. I barely noticed. I hitched up my skirt, moving to pull my underwear down, and felt him grasp me tightly by the wrist. He looked down at me with a mixture of sadness and anger. "I said no," he growled, breathing hard.

He stood, leaving me shaking on the floor, half dressed and wild eyed. "I'm going to bed. I suggest you sleep in the spare room. We'll discuss our options another time when you're less..." he shook his head, turned and walked out of the room. He hadn't reached the bottom of the stairs before I crumpled into a ball and wept.

Chapter Seven

"Do you think he really means it then?" Isabel said as she dipped her third biscuit into her tea and brought the soggy tip to her lips, a habit that made my stomach turn. After giving her and Bonnie the cold shoulder for longer than I had ever managed before, I'd finally backed down. I was desperate for someone to talk to.

"It's been two weeks, Issy. Two weeks of me begging him to reconsider and so far, he's not budged an inch. I don't know what I can do to make him change his mind," I complained, leaning back in the squashy armchair in her living room. The seat was perfectly positioned so that I could see the corner of my own cul-de-sac through the bay windows, and I glanced in that direction now, wondering how long it would be until Lucas would come home. He'd been going to the pub after work most nights this past fortnight, or making excuses for why he had to stay late at the surgery. He was avoiding me, I knew he was, and I couldn't blame him.

For the first week after that frightful dinner, I had been relentless in my desperation. I'd refused to let the subject go for even a second. I'd been humiliated beyond words when a further two attempts to seduce him, both far less frenzied and in my opinion, infinitely more difficult to resist than the kitchen fiasco, had both gone rebuffed. I'd sobbed into my lacy black lingerie, drinking the champagne alone by candlelight, as he had gone out for a drink with his friend Ben from Uni. To talk about me, no doubt. I'd been furious, hurt, and utterly despairing, and several blazing rows had erupted in the days that followed.

The second week however, I had calmed down a little. During one of my endless, insomnia ridden nights, while pacing the living room floor, no doubt wearing holes in the already threadbare carpet, I'd suddenly realised I was making it all so much worse. By acting so manically I was pushing him further away rather than pulling him back to me. I was cementing his decision, proving his concerns that I wasn't strong enough to go through another pregnancy. Another potential loss.

If I was going to have any chance of swaying his

decision, I needed to back off for a while. What we needed was fun. Time to laugh and be silly and remember why we fell in love in the first place. We needed to get rid of the stress and just be Roxy and Lucas again. Only, that plan wasn't working so well either. Lucas had hardly been home all week, and on the two nights he had made an appearance, he'd baulked at the idea of spending any time together, convinced that I was up to no good and trying to change his mind again. He'd even refused to watch a martial arts film with me, taking himself off to bed, leaving me feeling rejected and lonely downstairs. I was missing him dreadfully.

Isabel put her mug down on the table and screwed up her face. She looked so young when she did that. It was hard to believe that she was a grown up now, in a serious grown up job. But social work suited her. Though Isabel had a tendency towards fretting and anxiety in her personal life, caring for others was meditation to her. She remained a workaholic long after our mother's death, and now I believed it would always be a big part of who she was. She couldn't help it. She loved nothing more than taking on a massive, difficult case, and finding a solution.

Where some people would have gossiped about the children they met, their unfortunate circumstances and the abuse they had suffered, Isabel never had. She treated each and every one of them with respect, reverence even, and held their secrets just as tightly as she kept her own. She loved her work, and I knew she thought of it as a blissful release from her own worries. As great as she was with strangers' issues though, she hated to be brought into family squabbles. Being put smack bang in the middle of my marital troubles was nothing short of a nightmare for her, and I could see that the situation was making her uncomfortable.

"I don't know what to say," she said softly now. "There doesn't seem to be a right answer, does there?"

I felt my eyes begin to sting as tears prickled beneath my lashes, and shook my head, swallowing thickly. "I just want a baby so badly, Issy. I want it so much I can barely breathe."

"I know. I know you do sweetie." Isabel moved to sit on the arm of my chair and put an arm around me.

We sat silently for a while, Isabel rubbing soothing circles on my back.

A sudden commotion from the opposite end of the house made us both jump up. I wiped my eyes hurriedly as the two of us rushed towards the banging, shrieking noises. We entered the kitchen to find Bonnie along with two very good looking men and a girl around Bonnie's age, holding on to each other and laughing uncontrollably. The men broke free, one swinging a bag which clinked with glass bottles up onto the kitchen side. "Bonnie Cormack!" shrieked Isabel! "What on earth is going on? You're wasted!"

Bonnie, smiling like a Cheshire cat, danced her way over to Isabel and I and pulled us both into a hug. "I'm not wasted! Plenty of time to get there though," she giggled. "It's Rex's birthday," she said, pointing towards the taller of the two men. He bowed in our direction on hearing his name, which made both Bonnie and the other girl break into peals of laughter, both offering deep courtesies in return.

Bonnie turned back to Isabel, grinning. "We're celebrating. Have a drink with us." The other man pulled several bottles of vodka from the bag and started pouring generous glugs into glasses on the counter. "This is Laura and Mike," Bonnie gestured, picking up two of the glasses and holding them out to Isabel and I, who both turned to look at each other with expressions of amusement. Bonnie was hilarious after a few drinks.

I gave an exaggerated shrug towards Isabel. "Well, why the hell not? It's not as if I'm pregnant, is it?" I said, my voice hitching as I took the glass and downed the heady beverage in one.

"Atta girl," Bonnie grinned, pushing the other glass into my hand and turning back to her friends. She hadn't seemed to pick up on the sadness behind my words. I watched her go, feeling a little unsettled. Bonnie always read between the lines. Isabel took my arm, her face creased in worry.

"Roxy? Should you, I mean... Is this a good idea?"

I shook my head. "Don't worry, Isabel. It's okay, honey. It is," I said, giving her a genuine smile. "Come on. If there's going to be a party, we may as well join in." Isabel chewed at her bottom lip for a moment, unmoving as she tried to work out what to do. "Please?" I said. "I need to have fun. I need this. I promise, I'll be okay." I held out the drink to her.

Isabel gave a short nod and took the glass. "If I'm sick tomorrow, you're getting the blame, you bad influence!" she smiled. Then she threw her head back, swallowing the burning alcohol in one go.

I couldn't remember the last time I'd had so much fun. There was music playing, someone had poured me a glass of wine, which I far preferred to the gluey taste of the vodka, and I was laughing until my ribs hurt with my sisters. Bonnie was dancing barefoot around the room, swaying between Rex and Mike who from the look of it were both equally besotted with her. I couldn't blame them, she was utterly magnetic. She'd always been able to captivate, to draw people into her little bubble. She oozed with a certain energy you just couldn't put your finger on, but it was undeniably there. Everyone loved Bonnie.

Her friend, Laura, was telling me and Isabel a story about an audition she'd had for the part of Mary Poppins for an amateur stage production, complete with impressions which had all three of us rolling around in fits of laughter. We were breathless with giggles as Laura exclaimed indignantly that she hadn't even had a call back. "Unbelievable," Isabel choked through a mouthful of lager. "You were robbed!"

I smiled around the room feeling relaxed and happy. It was somewhat unsettling to realise how long it had been since I had just laughed with my sisters. A gentle tapping at the window caught my attention and I looked up to see Lucas looking in at us. I gave a wave, smiling and gesturing for him to come inside, and then felt the nerves begin to bubble in my stomach again at the thought of being close to my husband. I didn't want to spoil tonight. I didn't want to argue.

Lucas strode into the room, his expression unreadable. "So here you are, you little runaway," he said. "I thought as much." He took a beer from Bonnie's proffered hand, casting his eyes around the room. "I wasn't expecting a party though."

"Birthday party!" slurred Bonnie, heading over to change the music from dance to reggae.

"So I see," Lucas said, his eyes on me, questioning and uncertain.

"You don't mind do you?" I asked, getting to my feet. "It's just, well, Bonnie said... I just wanted to have a bit of fun," I shrugged, aware that my speech was slurring a little. His mouth twitched, a smile tugging at its corners.

"Do you know how wonderful it was watching you through the window just then?" he asked softly, so only I could hear. He took my hand, pulling me closer to him. "I can't remember the last time I saw you laughing like that." He leaned down, his eyes on mine, deep pools of rich melting chocolate, and I felt my stomach jolt. This was my Lucas, the man I knew. The man who had swept me off my feet all those years back, and somehow managed to keep me there. He stroked my hair back from my face, his fingertips cool against my skin. "Of course I don't mind." He leaned down and kissed me and I melted into him without hesitation.

"Oh get a room!" Isabel laughed merrily.

Lucas lifted his head to look up at his sister-in-law with a grin. "I'll take a dance instead," he winked.

*

"We should've at least eaten dinner," Lucas laughed as we weaved our way across the green that led to our house.

"Beer counts as dinner," I retorted. "I read that it's pretty much liquid bread, chock full of carbs!" I slurred, leaning into him. My feet were bare and I looked down at them, realising with a giggle that I'd left my shoes behind. Never-mind. Lucas stopped walking suddenly and I wondered if he was going to puke. "You okay?" I asked, stopping too. Instead of being sick though, he looked up to the night sky, staring at the stars.

"Beautiful, aren't they?" he whispered. He turned his attention to me, his eyes intense as they met my own. "Not the most beautiful thing I can see though... not by a long way." I stared up at him, seeing the man I knew so well, my Lucas, my big strong sensitive husband. I was so happy to have him back, to have him look at me with so much warmth and emotion. I loved him so much. The night air was crisp and cool, and I leaned closer into him, soaking up his warmth. "God I've really fucking missed you,

Roxy. You have no idea how much," he said, his voice deep and smooth.

"I've missed you too. I'm so sorry I checked out like that. I'm sorry, Lucas."

"I'm sorry too."

I saw tears in his eyes and realised I was crying too. And then, his mouth was on mine, fierce and fast and hot, and we were reaching beneath each others clothes, both moving across the cold, dewy grass towards our front door. Our hands didn't leave each other as we burst through the door and fell in a tangle of limbs and discarded clothes onto the hallway carpet. Lucas kicked the front door shut behind him, then there was nothing but darkness and pleasure.

Chapter Eight

Four months later.

"You look... beautiful," Lucas said, his eyes trained on me as I tied the belt of my wrap-around dress. My hair was still cocooned within a turban of an emerald green towel, and I had yet to put on a scrap of make up. I raised a quizzical eyebrow at him and pursed my lips. "Enough with your empty flattery! Get up or we'll be late," I ordered, unwinding the towel and tossing it in his direction.

He caught it deftly and grinned. "I'm serious. You do look beautiful." I shook my head, a smile tugging at the corners of my mouth, and turned to stare at my reflection in the mirrored wardrobe door. There it was. Undeniably, indisputably and yes, I had to agree, beautifully present. A bump.

I placed my hands on my hips, marvelling at my swollen, protruding abdomen. In all my pregnancies I had never reached the stage where I'd had a bump. Visual proof that my body was growing a tiny person.

Sustaining life. Holding on. "It *is* beautiful, isn't it?" I murmured softly, my hands running over the convex surface of my belly. "Glorious."

As if responding to the compliment, a thrumming of kicks volleyed against my palm, followed by a slow roll as the baby changed position. "Good morning, sweet angel," I whispered, fearful that my voice was causing the little being to fret.

"Come here," Lucas smiled, still watching me. He held out his arms expectantly and I walked around the bed, perching beside him.

"I can't believe we're going to see our baby today. We're going to find out if we're having a boy or a girl. A son or a daughter!" I exclaimed, breathless with excitement. I didn't want to think about the possibility that we would also find out if there was something wrong. An anomaly scan, they had called it. Though this was in fact my sixth pregnancy, this would be the first twenty week scan I would have the privilege to attend, and I wasn't at all sure what to expect. Would they tell me that something was horribly amiss? Somehow, I just couldn't believe that to be possible. Not this time. Not this baby.

Everything had been so different about this pregnancy, even right at the beginning. I hadn't even had to do a test to prove it to myself, I had just known with a deep, unquestioning certainty that I was carrying a new life inside me. This time, my symptoms had been obvious. The sickness and nausea had consumed my days for the whole of the first trimester. My breasts had swollen to larger than they'd ever been, and were so tender that even the slightest touch could make me gasp with pain. I'd never felt so utterly, intensely pregnant. I could feel the strength of the little soul inside me. I could feel everything changing and transforming within my body. I was going to get to meet this one, I just knew it.

And now, feeling my baby kick and move within me, secure in the knowledge that a little heart continued to beat strongly twenty weeks on, I felt hope. More than that, I felt sure. This baby would survive. I *would* hold this child. I *would* be a mother. I leaned forward, kissing Lucas softly on the lips before pulling back. "Get up, cheeky, we have to go. The scan is in an hour."

"We have time."

"How can you even think of – *that!* – when we get to see our baby today? I'm so excited I can barely think straight."

"So, you need a distraction," he said, pulling himself upright and grabbing my arm playfully, guiding me back down towards him. He kissed the spot behind my ear, his stubble rubbing against the smooth skin, and I shuddered with pleasure. I was so damn sensitive these days, and he knew it.

"You're taking advantage of me," I laughed, as I let him guide me onto the bed.

"Let me distract you," he whispered as he lowered his mouth to mine.

"You have twenty minutes," I warned, drawing in a breath as his hand slipped beneath the cotton of my underwear.

He chuckled, his breath hot against my throat. "Who says romance is dead?" he murmured. I gasped, my head sinking blissfully into the pillow, surrendering to my husband's touch.

The waiting room was humming with the buzz of

couples itching to be seen, others having already had their scan brimming with joy, discussing the new life they were bringing into the world. I held onto Lucas's hand tightly as I watched everyone, my excitement turning to nerves now. What if I was wrong? What if the baby wasn't okay and we were about to find out we were losing another child? I couldn't bear it. I watched a couple coming out of one of the side doors now, shocked expressions on both of their faces. "Twins!" I heard the man exclaim. "Bloody twins," he repeated with a shake of his head.

The woman smiled. "I know," she replied. "We're so lucky." The man coughed and went a shade of white that had me concerned, and then, before I could jump up to help, he swayed, grabbed for the desk, missed and fell onto the ground in a heap. "He's fainted!" the woman shrieked. "Somebody help!" People were already crowding around the inert lump, attempting to roll him, nurses trying to push their way through to assist. I watched it play out, fascinated. There was a tug at my hand and I looked round to see Lucas staring at me.

"What?"

"They called your name. It's our turn," he said, getting to his feet. I stood slowly and looked at the nurse in the doorway across the room, tapping her pen impatiently against her clipboard. I suddenly felt like I might be next to faint. I took a deep breath and swallowed. Lucas nodded reassuringly, and I saw a flash of fear in his eyes, but then he blinked and it was gone, and I was being led across the crowded room whether I was ready or not. I made an indistinct sound in the back of my throat as the nurse confirmed my identity and then followed her into the darkness of the room, my grip on my husband's hand never easing for even a second.

"A boy!" Lucas shouted, pounding his fist in the air as he paced on the patch of grass outside the hospital. "We're having a boy!" he roared. I could hardly believe it. The scan had been over in a matter of minutes and we had been told we were having one very healthy, very wriggly, baby boy. My face felt like it would split in two, my heart was fluttering like a butterfly. It was really happening. I was carrying a son. My son. My baby boy. It sounded so wonderful.

I watched Lucas literally jumping for joy, laughing as I pictured his big strong arms wrapping our son up safe and warm. I pictured our baby's face, knowing it was only a matter of months before we would meet him. I had never felt so happy in my whole life.

And then, before I understood what was happening, my laughter transformed and I was sobbing, collapsing into the grass, feeling the weight of Lucas's body wrapping itself against mine as he rushed to hold me. I hadn't realised how scared I was, how much tension I had been holding onto until I learned that my baby was safe.

Relief poured out of me now, my sobs carrying away months and years of loss and pain. Making way for something new and fresh and beautiful. Those pregnancies would never, could never, be forgotten. Those babies that never made it would always be a part of me. But now it was time to stop looking backwards. To let the hurting fade. Now I needed to look to my future. I was going to have a son.

Chapter Nine

I smiled to myself as I squatted to check on the chicken roasting in the oven. It had been two days since the scan and I had somehow managed to resist telling Isabel and Bonnie the good news that I was at last pregnant for keeps. *Not good news, great news,* I thought. *No, bloody wonderful, brilliant, stupendous news, in fact.*

They knew. Of course they knew! Despite living in baggy t-shirts and oversized jumpers, I'd suspected that Bonnie had seen it from day one, her ever watchful gaze taking in the subtle changes only she would see. Her eyes dull, her face creased with worry, waiting for what by now had become the inevitable. She'd been unable to resist watching me as the weeks had passed. Fidgeting, hinting heavily, visiting daily, ready to offer comfort to me and Lucas when the tides turned, to feel like she was helping in some small way. I was used to the intensity of her caring. The way she smothered me with her love in an attempt to hide her own hurting.

As the pregnancy had progressed however, Bonnie's expression had transformed into one of surprise, mingled with tentative hope. I could sense the flood of unanswered questions desperate to pour from her lips. I knew she was rooting for me, for the child. I knew that she had seen the secret I was hiding even before my own husband had realised the truth.

I would've liked to be able to talk to her, to share how I was feeling, the certainty that this time it was different, but I hadn't found the courage to do it. I didn't want to put words to it, to put any pressure on myself. To have to break their hearts all over again if I was wrong. It was too much responsibility to bear. So I had kept my secret, and to her credit and no doubt Isabel's too, they had resisted the urge to question or congratulate. They knew the ball had to be in my court for this. They had to wait.

I'd kept my secret so well protected, that I'd only made the decision to open up to Lucas on the day of my twelve week scan. To begin with, I had planned to go alone, it felt better not to bring him, to put him through it all over again. But then, something magical had happened which had changed my mind in an instant. It had been tiny, a sensation as delicate as a butterfly's wings, a pop and a flutter. It was the unmistakable movement of something dwelling deep within me. My baby was alive and stretching out, sending me a message that everything was going to be okay. The unexpected stirring had reduced me to tears. Lucas had walked into the bedroom to find me sobbing, laughing, hysterical with the brilliance of it, and finally ready to let him in.

There was a knock on the kitchen door now, and I turned with a smile as Bonnie came in from the garden, kissing me on the cheek. "Hi babe, how are ya?" She pulled up a stool at the breakfast bar as I flicked the kettle on to boil.

"I'm okay," I smiled, noticing the dark circles beneath my sister's eyes. "You want a cup?"

She shrugged. "I'd prefer something a little stronger." She gave a smile, but I noticed it didn't quite reach her eyes. For a moment, I didn't move, I simply stared at her, wondering what was different. How long had it been since I had really taken in her appearance? Weeks? Months? God knew I'd been so wrapped up in myself I'd neglected to be there for everyone else, Bonnie included. But now I looked, really looked I was shocked at what I saw. Dark circles beneath her eyes, a defeated slump to shoulders that had always been so strong. Though she had always been slim, I saw now that she had lost even more weight. Her cheeks looked hollow, she was more gaunt than slender. The way she moved gave no evidence of the woman who had once been so alive and full of energy and passion for life. Bonnie was struggling.

"Uh, Rox... do you want me to get the drink?" she asked now, raising her brows quizzically at me. I stepped forward, leaning over the counter and taking her hand, squeezing it tightly.

"What's happened, Bon? What's happened to you?" I asked, my voice quiet, urgent. She blinked, and pulled her hand back abruptly, shaking her head.

"I brought beer," she said in response, opening the drawer and helping herself to a bottle opener.

"Bonnie," I urged softly, watching as she flipped the shiny metal top off the bottle. It hit the tile with a chink. Neither of us moved to pick it up. She drank deeply, wiped her mouth on the back of her sleeve and looked up at me.

"What do you want me to say?" she asked, meeting my eyes. "I'm fine. Really Sis."

I shook my head, wondering if she was telling the truth. Everything about her appearance screamed otherwise, but then, surely if something was going on I would know? Isabel would know, and Lucas too, even if I had been too wrapped up in my own problems. "Are you?"

"Yes."

"You're sure?"

"I'm sure. And I think your potatoes are boiling over."

"Oh shit!" I rushed over, turning the gas down and moving the pan aside. I turned back to see Bonnie heading down the hall into the living room. I didn't follow.

An hour later my home was buzzing with the chatter of my family. I looked around happily, watching Lucas chatting to Isabel. Bonnie had joined us again and seemed to have cheered up. I decided I was making drama out of nothing. She was probably just tired. A little run down, that was all.

"Dinner's not quite ready," I called over the noise of the chattering. "Why don't you all head into the living room and make yourselves comfortable in there while I finish up? Here," I added, pushing a bottle of red into Bonnie's hand. "Take this."

"You not having a glass with us, Sis?" she asked loudly, her eyes twinkling mischievously.

"Uh, no, not right now," I replied, feeling my face flush as she scrutinised me. The room went silent and I heard Isabel give a tinkling giggle.

"Any particular reason why not?" Bonnie asked, sounding on the verge of laughter herself. I looked over at Lucas for help, my eyes wide and panicked, and he responded by giving a shrug and a grin.

"Go ahead, darling, you may as well spill the beans."

I looked around the room at the smiling, expectant faces of my siblings. "Well, you've both bloody guessed by now, no doubt, but, yes, I'm pregnant! Twenty weeks. And it's a boy!" I shrieked, overcome with elation now. Bonnie gave a delighted whoop and then all at once, two pairs of arms descended on me and Lucas, distributing hugs, patting my bump, slapping Lucas firmly on the back.

"Well, of course we guessed," said Bonnie, "but we had no idea it was a boy! Oh you two are going to have a little baby. I'm going to be an Auntie! I'm over the moon for you, really I am!" She wrapped Lucas in a tight hug. I was grinning from ear to ear. How good it felt to finally have some positive news to share. How wonderful to see the happy smiling faces of my sisters after all the heartache that had passed. I felt my son turn and roll within my womb and wrapped my arms around myself, sure I would burst with the joy of it.

Isabel slipped into the kitchen, her heels clicking against the tile. She came to a stop behind me as I was pulling the cutlery from the drawer and wrapped her arms around my belly, giving a gentle squeeze. I turned and returned the hug.

"Oh, Rox. I'm so happy for you. And for Lucas," Isabel smiled. "You've waited so long for this. And you've both been through so much. It's broken my heart to see you so sad and not be able to help. We all feel your pain. You know how much we love you," she said, her eyes shimmering with unspilled tears. "You really do deserve some good luck. I'm so glad things are finally working out for you."

I smiled into her hair and sighed. "I'm happy too. A little scared, I'd be crazy not to have niggles after, well, you know... but I really feel like this is going to end well. I can feel him moving all the time. He's strong, and it's different this time. My body feels different. It's hard to explain."

"You don't have to. Just enjoy it," she smiled running a hand through her mane of red curls, re-pinning a strand that kept falling into her eye. "Have you thought of any names?"

"Not yet. I want to wait until we see his face, see who he looks like."

"That's a good idea," she nodded. She turned and absent mindedly picked up a cloth, wiping it over the already sparkling sink. I paused, watching her closely. Her face was fixed in a relaxed expression, but there was something else in her eyes. Something was off.

"Isabel, what's wrong?"

Isabel stopped wiping and looked up, her sparkling

green eyes meeting my own. She gave a sigh and dropped the cloth, taking me by the hand. "It's not the right time. I don't want to spoil your celebration."

"Issy, this is me. You can tell me anything. It won't spoil a thing! Please, what is it?"

She sighed again. "Come and sit down." She squeezed my hand, and walked over to the half set table. I followed silently, pulling out a chair to sit beside her and looking at her with concern. She twiddled a napkin between her fingertips, and it seemed she was suddenly lost for words.

"Well, what is it?" I pushed feeling a flush of impatience mingled with fear.

"I didn't want to have to tell you, but she won't listen to me. I'm getting worried." She dropped the napkin back on the table and lifted her face. "Rox, it's Bonnie."

"Bonnie? What about her?"

"She's in trouble. She hides it well, but..."

I felt my stomach drop. She wasn't okay, I should have listened to my instincts. "What kind of trouble? Money?"

"No." She looked away, uncomfortably. "She's

been, ah, I don't know how to say this. I didn't want to have to, but I really am worried."

"What is this, Issy? What's going on?"

Isabel pursed her lips and met my eyes. "She's been drinking. A lot. And there have been other things too. Drugs... Men."

"Are you serious?" I laughed. "No. Bonnie wouldn't do that. I know she's been drinking more than she should, but drugs? No. She just wouldn't do that."

"I didn't realise how bad it was either, Rox. It's only since she's been living with me that I've seen it. She's out every night. She sleeps till after lunchtime. And she's been having terrible mood-swings. She broke my television. Put her foot right through the screen. I'm not kidding, Rox."

"How could you have kept this to yourself, Issy, how could you not tell me?"

"You've been going through a lot, we all know it. The last thing I would want is to add to your worries, it wouldn't be fair. But this isn't something that's just a one off. It's been going on a long time. You know she's never been the same since mum died." She picked up the napkin again, folding and unfolding it, balling it in the palm of her hand. "She never properly grieved. She's still so raw from it all," she added sadly. "She won't talk to me. And she's trying to numb it in all the wrong ways. I'm scared for her. I really am. I don't want to lose her too."

I felt utterly floored. How could I not have seen my sister's pain? How could I have neglected to notice her descending into alcoholism? And *drugs?* I would never have believed it possible. She may have had a wild side, and I knew she loved to party, but I couldn't fathom her being so reckless that she would turn to drugs. But perhaps Isabel was right. Bonnie had always had a secretive side, an air of mystery about her. Perhaps she was better at hiding the truth than I'd ever realised. And through it all, she had never even come to me. I felt sick at the thought of her in pain with nobody to turn to. I should have been there for her, not so wrapped up in my own despair, my own loss.

Bonnie had always been particularly close to our mother. During her illness, she'd been the one to hold on tight to the hope that she was coming back to her.

She had never let that dream go, even when things became really bad. And when Rosie was so strung out she could barely recognise the rest of us, she always knew her Bonnie. She always came back, that tiny bit, just for her. There had been something special between them, so it was little surprise that she had felt most betrayed when mum had killed herself. It had been devastating for the whole family, but Isabel and I had already grieved the loss of our mother, long before she killed herself. She hadn't been the person we knew and loved for several years. Inch by inch we had let her go, knowing that we had lost the battle. Bipolar had consumed her until there was nothing left.

Isabel took my hand now, seeing my pale, drawn face. "It will be okay Sis. We will help her, together. We will bring her out of this mess."

I just nodded and hoped it wasn't too late.

I pushed back my chair and went to the oven, pleased to see the perfect golden crust on the apple pie. "It's ready," I announced to the laughing rambunctious crowd around the table. My eyes flicked to Bonnie who was telling a story to the family, laughing as she spoke. She looked so alive, so vibrant. Seeing her like this made it hard to believe things were as bad as Issy had made out. The lunch had gone smoothly, everyone smiling and talking about the pregnancy that was no longer taboo. I had found myself swept up with the celebratory atmosphere, despite my concerns over Bonnie.

"Here, let me help you with that," Lucas said, jumping up from his seat.

"No, no, you sit down. I've got it," I insisted, leaning into the oven and easing the desert out. I stood up, catching the inside of my forearm on the edge of the tin. A white hot pain shot through my arm and I automatically released the pie with a yell as I grabbed for my singed flesh. It crashed to the ground, splattering pieces of hot apple and pastry all over the tile. "Shit!"

"Are you okay? Let me have a look," Lucas insisted, taking my arm in his big warm hands to inspect the damage. There was a large red welt running horizontally across my skin. "Here," he said, pulling me towards the sink. I winced as he turned the cold tap on and ran the water, guiding my arm gently beneath it."

"What a waste of a good pudding," I mourned sadly, my stomach growling at the thought of it. I'd been craving sweet apple pie all day.

"I'm more worried about you," Lucas frowned, still holding my arm under the water. It stung.

"I'm fine. It only caught me for a second, should have used the gloves instead of the tea-towel." I pulled my arm out of the flowing water and appraised it. "See, it's fading already." I kissed him. "I'm going to pop out and get another pie."

"Don't be silly, Rox!" called Isabel. "We'll do without it."

"No, I want pie. I *need* apple pie."

"I'll go then," Bonnie said, standing up.

"No, you won't. You've all been drinking. As if I'm going to let any of you drive anywhere!" I laughed. "It's fine, I'll go and get another one. Sit down. I'll be back before you even miss me." I picked up my bag, blew a kiss to the room, and left before anyone else could argue with me.

I was actually glad to have an excuse to get a few

minutes on my own. I needed to think. The lunch had been lovely, finally being able to speak openly about the pregnancy, to share our joy and talk about the future with hope for the first time in many years. I was feeling good. But I was also tired. A symptom of growing new life, I knew, but it felt nice to take a quiet drive down to the shops and collect my thoughts.

Isabel and I had decided to talk privately to Bonnie the following day. Neither of us wanted to make a scene over a nice family lunch, and after I'd had time to consider the situation, I had felt certain that I could get her to open up to me and let out all those toxic emotions she was holding onto. I smiled, sure that everything was going to work out okay. It was time for everyone's luck to change, and I had proved that by finally holding onto my baby.

I wound down the window, letting the cool air filter through the car, the smell of leaves and grass and damp filling my nostrils. It had rained during lunch and I breathed in deep, savouring the smell of wet earth, enjoying the crisp, clean aftermath of the storm. It was one of my favourite smells in the whole world.

The wonderful thing about living in Oxford was that if you knew the right places, you could feel like you were right in the countryside. I always took the back-roads and little lanes when I drove anywhere. I preferred to walk though. I liked to discover little pathways through fields, or stroll along the River Thames, avoiding the crowds as much as was possible in a city. It was such a beautiful place to live, truly the best of both worlds. The burn on my arm tingled a little as I flicked the indicator to turn left towards the shops, manoeuvring my Mini into the narrow lane. Rounding the corner, I decided I would run it under the tap again for a few more minutes when I got back. Couldn't hurt to be extra cautious.

As I straightened the car into the road, I was suddenly torn from my thoughts, my body thrown into autopilot, my mind instantly analysing and assessing the situation surrounding me. A truck was speeding towards me, skidding and swerving in and out of my lane with no sign of stopping. All at once, everything became very clear. To the left there was nothing but a narrow ditch and a thick hedge. There was no space to pass on the right. And the truck driver was not going to stop. Something was very wrong.

My arms moved, my hands gripping tightly to the wheel as I swerved towards the ditch, reasoning it was my best option. As the left hand side of the Mini hit the verge, the wheels sank into the soft sticky mud and the car was upended diagonally, the right hand side sticking up, the wheels spinning against thin air. I grasped the steering wheel, breathing hard and saw with utter terror the wide axle of the truck heading right for me.

There was a scream, an explosive crunch of metal on metal, shattering glass, and I was flung forwards, backwards, forwards again. My head hit the wheel and blood poured hot and metallic into my eyes and mouth. A pain shot through my leg and my ear simultaneously and I felt as if my eyes might burst out of my skull. I let out a blood-curdling scream and wrapped my arms around my belly. "Please don't leave me baby," I croaked, "Please don't go."

I fought the pain, resisting where it was taking me, sure that if I let go I wouldn't make it back. I had to live. I had to protect my baby. My mind swam. There was nothing but pain, so much pain. I was drowning in it, consumed in agony. The smell of blood and smoke surrounded me and I wondered if the car was alight. Would I be cremated in my seat? It would mean an end to this torture, this unbearable misery. I choked and vomited into my lap. And then, the edges of the world faded out and there was only darkness.

Chapter Ten

There was light flashing on and off behind my closed eyelids. Voices, shouting, screaming. I couldn't breathe, my eyes wouldn't open, the pain was still there, worse now. I hadn't thought it possible, but it was. I must be dying. I had to be. I slipped out of consciousness again, and when I came round after what could have been minutes or hours, I was still in the same place.

Someone was calling me. It sounded far off, echoey, my own name bouncing around the darkness of my mind. I forced open an eye and saw a blurred face, familiar somehow. Ray. My neighbour. Why was he here? Was he looking at me through the roof? Everything was upside down, I didn't understand. "Lucas," I croaked. "Get Lucas."

"I'll go, I'll get him. The paramedics are pulling up now, they'll take care of you, Roxanne. Don't move."

My eyes flickered closed again and I heard more voices. Were they talking to *me*? It was fuzzy. I couldn't focus, the pain was too much, it burned through me though I couldn't muster the strength to scream again.

"Roxanne," a woman's voice said, closer than I thought possible. "I'm Sara, I'm a paramedic. Can you hear me?"

I tried to reply, but nothing came out. I could no longer open my eyes. With every ounce of strength I could muster I croaked out one word. "Baby."

"There's a baby in the car?" Sara tried to confirm.

"P... Pr... Pregnant," I managed to whisper, realising my arms were still wrapped around my abdomen.

"You're pregnant," Sara confirmed. "Thank you. We're here for you, Roxanne. We just need to get you out of here, then you and your baby will be treated. Try to stay as still as possible while we work around you. Can you tell me what hurts?"

I didn't understand the question. The pain was everywhere, burning, stinging, slicing. The sensation behind my eyes and in my ears felt as if something was going to explode, the pressure was incomprehensible.

"Head," I managed, though there was so much

more. I could feel the strength leaving me in increments. My body was going into emergency shut down. I could feel a numbness in my toes, my calves burning and tingling. My heart was beating hard enough to burst.

I realised with sickening clarity that my son, my precious baby was going to die. My body was doing everything it could to keep me alive. It would shut him off. It would take everything he needed to survive and give it to my vital organs instead. I was going to lose him and there was nothing I could do to stop it. I would have torn out my own heart in that very moment if it would have kept him safe.

"Okay," Sara continued, oblivious to my heartbreak. "Keep nice and still. I'm going to stay right here." I heard more people coming, unfamiliar noises, the scraping and cutting of metal. The sounds sliced through my brain, searing, unbearable. I shook my head, trying to block it out. Behind my eyelids everything flashed again, frenzied, nausea inducing. I was spinning, falling, it was too much.

The voices grew distant again, the echo was back. Nothing made sense. The flashing faded, and my head lolled back against the headrest, my mouth falling open as consciousness left me.

Chapter Eleven

There was no slow dawning of realisation on awakening. At the first trickle of consciousness, before my eyes had even peeled themselves open, two thoughts flashed brutally, crisply through my mind. Car crash. Baby gone. My insides tangled into a burning mass, fat snakes coiling and sliding inside my abdomen spilling their venom on everything they touched, burning a hole through the heart of me.

The loss was harsher than any that had come before it. The injustice too much to bear. I would have preferred a few moments of groggy, blissful ignorance. Amnesia would have been a welcome gift to dull the pain. I didn't want to remember. To know how close I had come to holding my baby in my arms before having him cruelly snatched away from me. Of all the babies I had loved and carried within me, however briefly, I knew that this would be the one that would haunt me forever. My son. My boy. My eyes remained closed. I wasn't ready to face the world without him. I might never be.

I could still picture his fragile little face on the black and white scan photo. The soft, pursed lips, the tiny shell like ears. His hands had been balled tightly against his sides and I had imagined slipping my finger into his grasp, stroking the silky smooth, delicate skin coating his knuckles with the pad of my thumb, as he fed at my breast. So close. So very close.

Without willing it, a sound turned over deep within me, building and rolling its way up through my chest until it burst free. A keening, other worldly wail. Animal. Ghostly. Yet it seemed that I was connecting to something deeply human. Something primal. The oldest pain in the world, that of a woman losing her child. An unbearable yearning that could be understood only by a mother. But I would never be a mother. Not really.

The sorrowful howling, interwoven with pained shrieking continued to escape from my lips. I wanted it to stop but I was powerless to control the emotions that were pouring unrestrained from me. It was as though I were not of my body, but instead a silent, helpless witness torn between empathy and disgust.

Stop it. Stop this wretched noise. Pull yourself

together! I wanted to cry. But I couldn't stop. Instead it built louder, deeper, my eyes still squeezed tightly shut, unwilling to face my harsh, empty reality. There was nothing left for me now.

A door slammed open, hitting something solid with a crash and a familiar voice – my husband's voice – cried out my name in panic.

"Roxy! Darling, Rox, it's me! Sweetheart, it's Lucas! Please stop screaming. Please!" I felt him grab me by the shoulder, shaking lightly before letting go, but I still couldn't step into my body and do what needed to be done to stop the despairing wails.

"Stop!" he shouted now. "Roxy, stop this! Look at me, darling. Fuck! I only left you for a second. Would you just stop screaming?" I felt strong hands grip the tops of my arms and pull me upright into a sitting position. I fought against the force, struggling to get away, to retreat back into my isolation. I did not want to be helped. It was far too late for that.

Suddenly, hot, full lips met my own, stifling the unbearable sound that was pouring from them with a pressure I was too shocked to resist. Startled, my eyes flew open, staring into the deep brown gaze of my husband. He stared back, his mouth still covering mine, a bandage to my invisible wounds. Slowly, as if afraid he would set off the screams again, he pulled back, centimetres at a time. He gave a tiny shake of his head. "Bloody hell, Roxy," he said, breathless and shaken. "What on earth was that? You scared me half to death!" He laid me gently back against the pillows and rubbed the heel of his palm against his brow, before taking a deep, steadying breath.

I tried to move, to roll over, but found myself tangled in wires. Something was throbbing uncomfortably at my wrist, and with exploratory fingers, I followed a trailing wire from the source of discomfort and along the bed. Through bleary eyes I noted a bulging bag of yellowish fluid hanging from a cold grey drip stand. My head throbbed, and a sick, trembly feeling engulfed me, pulling me back towards the blissful release of unconsciousness.

Despite my desire for escape, I fought against it, willing myself to stay awake. Dragging my hand from the thin tubing that was connected to my vein, I let it travel slowly until it reached my stomach. I felt desperately for what I had lost. My baby. Numbness took over as I gently ran my fingers over the still swollen mass of my abdomen. It would take time for that to go, for my body to erase the traces of this horror.

"Roxy?"

I turned my head ever so slightly towards Lucas, a sad resignation sweeping over me now. He leaned forward and kissed me on the forehead, more gently this time. "God, you scared me then, Rox. How do you feel?"

I shook my head. How did I even begin to answer that question? I felt like dying. I wished I had. It would have been easier. His cool hand swept across my cheek, gently brushing my hair back from my face. "It's okay, sweetheart. Don't try to talk." He pursed his lips before continuing on. "You've been in an accident. You're in hospital. Don't worry, Rox, I'm right here with you. Isabel has been here day and night too, she just had to pop home for a moment. I'm sure she'll be here soon." I wondered why he didn't mention Bonnie. Had she come too? Was she waiting to see me? I couldn't find the strength to ask.

Slowly I lifted a hand to my throat, rubbing at it.

"Wa... wate..."

"Water?" he asked. I gave a tiny nod. He stood, walking around the bed and I heard the slow trickle of liquid being poured. Then he was back, softly lifting my head and placing a plasticy tasting straw between my lips. I took a tiny, tentative sip. The cool liquid rushed down my throat, soothing the rawness, burning slightly as it made contact. I took several more tiny sips, then turned my head, feeling Lucas lowering me back on to the pillow.

"Do you remember what happened?"

I lifted a hand and rubbed at my eyes, squinting as I tried to look at him. They hurt. My whole head throbbed, and I swallowed, trying to ignore the building nausea. "Turn the light off."

"It's not on. Wait though, I'll pull the blind down." I waited as he moved away from me, and then blissfully the unbearable brightness faded. Cautiously, I opened my eyes fully, coming to focus on my husband. "Thank you."

"Does the light hurt?"

"Yes. My head aches. How bad am I hurt?"

He sighed. "The accident was... Well, let's just say

you're not going to be driving that mini ever again. Do you remember anything?"

I peered at him. "The truck. It was coming right at me. I didn't have anywhere to go," I said slowly, the crash suddenly replaying brightly in my mind. My hands began to shake as I recalled the moment the vehicles made impact. That horrifying sound, the realisation that there was no way to avoid it. Lucas grabbed my hands in his own and squeezed tightly. "I'm so sorry, Lucas. I should never have gone," I whispered, tears fogging my vision.

"Hey, you did nothing wrong," he said, leaning forward and gently taking me in his arms. "You couldn't have known."

I shook my head. One wrong choice and I'd lost everything. And taken everything from Lucas too. I would never forgive myself for it. "What happened to... him?" I asked, needing to know where they had taken my son, wanting desperately to see him, just once.

"He didn't make it."

"I know, I'm not stupid. But..."

"He had a heart attack at the wheel. At least that

seems to be the general consensus. He was dead before the wheels stopped turning. I'm so sorry you had to go through that, sweetheart."

I shook my head. "I don't mean the driver," I said harshly, not caring that it made me sound callous. I couldn't think about him right now. "What happened to our baby, Lucas?" Tears sprang hot and fast from my eyes, streaming down my cheeks. "I need to see him. I have to," I rushed on, pushing the words out through choking, strangled sobs.

"Roxanne," Lucas breathed. "Oh, my darling, I'm sorry. I should have said. Of course I should have said, I'm such an idiot! He's still inside you. He's alive, darling, we didn't lose our baby. You kept him safe, Roxy," he smiled, his own eyes shining with unspilled tears.

"What?" I gasped, abruptly pulling my hands back from him and pushing them beneath my hospital gown. It couldn't be true. It couldn't.

"Truly. He's alive. They did an ultrasound yesterday. He's perfect. And strong."

"He's alive?" I sobbed. "I didn't lose him?"

"You didn't. We didn't."

My thoughts swam, dreamlike, confused and unsure. I couldn't bear to hope. With shaking fingers, I prodded my abdomen gently, and bit my lip as a firm kick responded to my intrusion. "He *is* alive!" I cried grabbing hold of Lucas's hand and guiding it to my belly so he could feel. "I can't believe he made it. Oh my sweet baby. Oh my strong little boy. I knew you were a fighter. I knew it!" Lucas held his palm over mine, and grinned as he felt the baby moving. "He's alive, he's alive, oh my baby," I laughed, tears streaming down my face. Lucas wrapped me in his arms as I let it sink in. I was still going to be a mother. It wasn't over. Not by a long shot.

Chapter Twelve

I must have fallen asleep again. When I woke, the pain in my head had subsided a little and I opened my eyes, relieved to find the light less assaulting to my senses. Lucas was sitting in an armchair, his head slumped forward, his mouth ajar, tiny snores escaping his lips. I smiled, watching the way the sun caught his dark hair, following the dust particles as they landed on him, soft and silent.

I looked down at the length of my body, wondering what I would find beneath the thin blue blankets. My right leg felt sore but something else was going on with the left one. It was stiff, unmoving, and far more painful than its partner. I eased the blanket back, peering beneath it and saw what I already half knew. My left thigh was swollen, thick black straps secured around it, a long white dressing covering what could only have been an incision wound. There were metal rods travelling down the length of my leg, forcing it to remain straight. Honestly, after the pain I'd felt in them at the scene of the crash, I was amazed I hadn't broken both of them. Or lost them.

Lucas stirred and then jolted up with a shout as if from a nightmare. He looked around wide eyed, then wiped his mouth and blinked. "Hey," he said, noticing I was awake.

"Hey."

His gaze ran down my body, pausing on my thigh. "Do you want me to tell you... about what happened?" I nodded. He stood up and came to sit on the edge of the bed, leaning over me to take a sip of water from the glass on the side table. He offered it to me and I shook my head. "You had a broken femur, dislocated knee, and a pretty serious concussion. Lots of other bumps, cuts and bruises too. They put you in a neck brace, but they said your spine is okay, so they took it off after a day."

"A day?" How long was I unconscious?"

"A little while." He dipped his head. "You were pretty in and out of it when they brought you in, but you talked a bit so they said it wasn't a coma, just a shut down response to the trauma. They did surgery on your leg the morning after, so yesterday, but I doubt you remember much of that? You've been getting a lot of morphine."

I shook my head. "I shouldn't have it – what about the baby?"

"Don't worry, Rox. Honestly, they know you're pregnant. They aren't doing anything they shouldn't." I frowned, not sure how much I trusted a bunch of strangers to make decisions for me and my baby, without me having the chance to research it first. "Anyway," he continued. "They had to put a pin in your thigh. It's going to take a while for you to be up on your feet again, but at least you're here."

"Yes... a pin? Like a metal one?"

"Yeah, why?"

"That's airport security screwed for the rest of our lives then!" I laughed. I couldn't manage to feel sorry for myself. I was alive, my baby was unharmed and I just had to endure a few weeks of bed-rest while my leg recovered. All in all it could have turned out a whole lot worse.

"They said if you didn't wake up properly today they would have to do some sort of scan on your head to check what was happening. They have a bit of a checklist. Vomiting, seizures, bleeding from the ears, and the like. They said you weren't showing signs of any sort of brain or skull injury. Just a concussion, so that's something, right? You probably won't have to have a scan now."

"That's good. Have you slept? Been home? Eaten?"

He took my hand, squeezing it. "Would you have in my situation?" His deep brown eyes met mine. "I've been fucking terrified, Roxy. I thought I was going to lose you. Both of you. Roy came bursting into the house like a wild animal, shouting about some accident, and it was like everything went into slow motion, at least for me. I didn't want to believe it was you he was talking about."

I squeezed his hand. "All for some apple pie, hey?" He twisted his mouth in a grim imitation of a smile. "What about my sisters? Are they okay?" He dropped my hand and I saw a flash of discomfort in his eyes. "Lucas?"

"Uh, well, Isabel has been here nearly as much as me. She's just popped out to get some lunch, I think. She'll be over the moon to see you awake again."

"And Bonnie?" I asked, feeling uneasy. I could

sense there was something big going on that he didn't want to tell me.

"We've all been so worried, Rox."

"Lucas!"

The door swung open and Isabel walked in, a brown paper bag swinging from her wrist, a cup of coffee in each hand. "You're awake!" she cried, seeing me sitting up in bed. She deposited her loot onto the table and leaned in to hug me. "Oh my god, Roxy, don't you ever scare us like that again. I thought we were..." I felt her shoulders slump against me and realised she was crying. "I thought we were going to... lose you," she finished in a choked whisper. I wrapped my arms around her, stroking her hair back from her face.

"You didn't. I'm still here, aren't I? I'm not going anywhere."

"You'd better bloody not. We've been in a right state, haven't we, Lucas?"

He nodded. Isabel handed him a coffee and he took it gratefully, moving back to the armchair by the window and sipping silently. "Do you want this one?" Isabel asked me, holding up the other cup. "I only got two, I thought you might still be, you know... sleeping."

I shook my head. The smell was revolting. "I don't think the baby likes coffee."

She put it back down again, pulling a paper-towel from the dispenser on the wall and wiping her eyes. She blew her nose loudly and threw it into the bin.

"Issy." She looked up, meeting my eyes. "Where's Bonnie?" A look of panic crossed her features. She turned to Lucas, and something passed between them that made me anxious. "Look, you don't have to protect me alright. I want to know what's going on. I deserve to know. Now tell me what's happened? Where is my sister?"

Lucas rubbed his eyes, letting out a low sigh. "We don't know. I'm sorry, Roxy, but she's... missing."

"What? What do you mean *missing*? How can she be?"

Isabel came back to the bed, perching on the end of it, careful not to touch my leg. "Okay... Look." She paused, glancing at Lucas who gave a resigned nod and took another sip of his drink. She turned back to me. "It took the emergency services a long time to get you out of that car," she began. "Roy told us where they were taking you, so me, Lucas and Bon jumped in his car and he dropped us off here. Only we got here before you."

"So?" I asked, irritated with how long it was taking for her to tell me what was going on.

"So we saw them bring you in. The paramedics. We saw you being wheeled in through A&E." She sighed and placed her hand over mine. "Rox, you looked bad. Really, really bad. Like, you might not make it bad, alright?" She winced at the memory and chewed her lip. "Bonnie was here, she was all ready to do the Florence Nightingale thing. But when she saw you," Isabel took a deep breath. "Well, she just lost it. She went white as a sheet and literally ran out. We were too busy worrying about you to go after her. I never thought she'd leave, I just thought she needed to take a minute."

"Have you called her?"

Isabel nodded. "Her phone's off. And..." she paused.

"And what?" I demanded. Isabel sighed and glanced at Lucas again. He stood up and came over to the bed, sitting opposite her, his hand running nervously up and down my blanket. "And what?" I almost shouted.

Isabel flinched. "I went home yesterday to get changed. Her stuff is gone. She's left, Roxy. She's just gone."

Chapter Thirteen

The news that Bonnie was missing had both frustrated and terrified me. Knowing what Isabel had told me about her recent behaviour, I felt an uneasy and constant bubble of panic over what she could be doing, where she might be. I'd sent Isabel to report her as missing to the police, but I knew they wouldn't take it seriously. She was an adult. And if she wanted to run away, she had every right to do so. And though she was acting reckless, partying and cutting herself off from her family like an angry teenager, the truth was, we didn't know enough to say whether she was struggling with her mental health. Neither Isabel nor I had mentioned our mum in the days following my accident, her mental health issues, the fact that Bonnie had always been the most similar, the most likely to fall off the rails of sanity. We didn't want to think about it.

I had convinced myself that I would find her, just as soon as I was able to get out of hospital and back on my feet again, but to my horror, the consultant had informed me on his ward round that not only would I have to be in hospital for a minimum of two weeks, but I would also need regular appointments with a physiotherapist to rehabilitate my leg. "To put it bluntly, Mrs. Bowen, this is no small injury. It is going to take months for you to recover fully." He had said if I responded well to the physio and practised daily I should be back to my full fitness by the time I reached thirty two weeks pregnant. "Of course, there are no guarantees," he'd cautioned sternly, his bedside manner lacking a certain amount of charm and positivity.

"But what am I going to do?" I complained to Lucas after the consultant had left. "I'm supposed to be working, saving for the baby. How can I be signed off work when I'm expecting to take maternity leave in a few months. It's not fair on the university, or my students."

He nodded, rubbing his stubbled chin with the palm of his hand. I had insisted he go home to shower and change his clothes, which he had done, but he hadn't wanted to waste time shaving, he'd told me. I planned to send him home to sleep tonight whether he liked it or not. He looked exhausted.

"I've been thinking about that since the surgeon explained the recovery timeline to me when we got here," he said, his voice slow, thoughtful. "I think you'll have to take early maternity leave. He said you would get a sick note to cover you until you're on your feet and able to cope again. Then you can go straight into your maternity leave."

"You mean, not go back at all? Stay off from now until the baby comes?"

"I know you love your job, and it's going to be sad to leave, but don't you think it's for the best? To rest, get back to your full health now before the baby arrives, without the worry of coming and going? Marking papers and giving lectures? I mean, I'll support you whatever you choose, but I'm just saying. It's an option."

"But what about money? Can we afford it?"

"We'll manage. If it's what you want to do, we'll figure it out."

I sat back against the plasticy hospital pillows, pondering his words. Could I do it? Leave my job now, not go back? I should have felt devastated at the prospect – my job had been my world for so long, it was my identity, my reason to get up in the mornings. But now? Now the thought of juggling all these balls, Bonnie, physio, the pregnancy... it seemed like too much. I was tired, though I hated to admit it. And now, I had a new purpose. The truth was, I didn't want to do it all. I wanted to be a mother. I wanted to be relaxed, to enjoy my pregnancy rather than endure it. And honestly, having waited so long to be in this position, I wasn't the least bit ashamed to admit that.

"Yes," I told him. "Yes. That *is* what I want. I can't deal with the stress of it all and it's not good for the baby. And if I leave now, my students can have a consistent teacher from now on." As I said the words I felt like a weight had lifted from my shoulders. I hadn't even realised how much I was worrying about it until the burden was lifted.

Lucas smiled and I saw his face relax as I gave him my answer. "Then it's done. Now we just have to figure out where your troublesome sister has absconded to, and we can finally have some peace," he grinned, raising an eyebrow.

"Why do I get the feeling that's not going to be a

simple task?"

The next two weeks passed with the speed of setting tar. Nothing at all happened for huge chunks of the day. Since I was taking early leave from work – something my superiors had taken with grace and understanding to my great relief – I had insisted Lucas go back to his job. One of us needed to bring in a full time wage to pay the bills. He had argued, but eventually given in, knowing that I was right. He would come to the hospital every evening straight after work, stopping on his way to pick up fruit, books, stir fried vegetables and whatever else I might be craving. But the days, when Isabel and Lucas were busy in the real world, and I was stuck alone in the stale, stuffy little hospital room, were *torture.*

I longed to get out of bed, to walk outside, breath in the fresh cool air. I fantasised about hiking, horse riding, swimming – anything physical, I just wanted so much to move, to get out of this little cell and live. Isabel had brought a journal in for me, and I used it to write list after list of the things I would do when I recovered. I wondered if I could take the baby on a kayak, how big he would have to be before we could take him camping. I wanted to do it all.

The long hours were broken up by the intermittent visits from the nurses, who I would talk to incessantly, relieved to have a friendly human face to chat to, if only for a few minutes. Even the brisk ones, the ones who made it absolutely clear they were far too busy to stand and chat, didn't escape my room without me forcing some words out of them. It didn't matter if they were grumpy, I was just elated that they were there. That I wasn't alone.

Every three days I had the absolute highlight of my week, the most interesting event on my calendar – my physio appointment. These, although exciting because it meant a trip out of my room, and more one on one attention with a real live person than I got during the rest of the day, were tinged with frustration and sadness. I was working so hard, trying my very best to get moving again, to do what I was instructed to do, but it was a slow, tiring process which more than once left me reduced to tears.

"Stop being so hard on yourself. It's one thing to try and push yourself, it's completely another to punish yourself for not making a miracle happen," Lorna had told me after I'd not managed to make it to the end of the ward hallway on her third visit. She was massaging my knee, slowly manipulating it to bend my leg, and I gritted my teeth, determined not to show her how much it hurt. She saw nonetheless, and reduced her movements. "Roxanne, you will get there. I know it's frustrating, but I promise, this is pretty much textbook. Give it another week and you'll be walking around, I'll bet you can even go outside. You just need to be patient. These things do take time."

"I know. I'm sorry, I just get so..."

"I know. I do understand."

I liked Lorna, not just because she broke the monotony of my days, but because she was genuinely kind. She clearly had a passion for her work, and that shone through. But as much as I wanted to believe her, as much as I hoped she was right, it was really hard to stay positive when our session had finished. I would go back to my quiet room, waiting for the clock to tick slowly around to the time when Lucas would come and save me from myself. I called

Bonnie's phone over and over again from my little prison, but it was always switched off. Isabel had been in touch with her band mates and the friends that she had contact details for, but nobody had seen her, or at least, nobody would admit to having seen her. It was a constant worry in the back of my mind, and part of me was furious at her for just disappearing without a trace. The police had said they were "looking into it," but it didn't seem to be making any difference.

And so the days crawled by. I doodled, read, stared out of the window and talked to my baby when I felt him moving. And slowly, just as Lorna had said I would, I began to get better. On my sixth session, I made it outside, standing in the rain, smiling like I'd just completed a triathlon, and feeling just as exhausted. On my next session I made it down to the small shop just outside the hospital. I bought myself a Crunchie and ate it on the bench outside, enjoying every single bite. And finally, four days after that, Lucas came in carrying two empty sports bags. He packed my things away, more haphazardly than I would have done, but I didn't care. I was going home. I bid goodbye to the nurses who had become friends to me during my stay, and I walked out of the hospital on my own two feet, determined I wouldn't be going back there for a very long time.

Chapter Fourteen

I pulled the tiny cotton baby-grows from the laundry basket, bringing each one to my nose, sniffing deeply before gently folding it. I placed each one in the drawer, knowing that the next time I would see it would be on my son. It had taken a long time for me to buy anything, let alone imagine it in use, but finally as I had made it to full term and the end of my pregnancy had come into view, I had accepted that I had made it this far without losing him, and something had changed inside me.

I'd been buying and washing and preparing like crazy in the last few days, and the house finally looked as though it were somewhere a baby might live. A little rocker sat in the corner of the bathroom, where I hoped the baby might sit or nap so I could shower, a row of sweet little animals on the bar which ran across it. I was filling up the drawer with clothes and hats and blankets, and I had even gone out and bought a car seat. It felt so good to see these things surrounding me.

I'd been signed off from the hospital four weeks previously, and though my leg was sometimes a little stiff in the mornings, it soon eased up and I was relieved to find I didn't seem to have any lasting damage from the break. I had bought Lorna flowers and chocolates, sad to say goodbye after she had given me so much support and encouragement during such a lonely period, and she had told me how proud she was of my determination to get moving again. I felt like I had a whole new lease of life, and I wanted to enjoy it.

Now as I bent over to put the last few bits in the drawer, I felt a sudden wave of blinding head-rush. I could hear the blood rushing in my ears, tiny white spots dancing in front of my eyes. I sank to my knees, breathing deeply, trying to shake it off. When it passed a few moments later a sharp pain stabbed just behind my ear. Another headache. I had been getting so many of them lately, but the midwife had assured me that my blood pressure was fine and it wasn't something to be concerned about. Seeing the bright blue cloudless sky out of the bedroom window, I decided I would make a cup of tea and sit in the fresh air until it passed.

It was peaceful in the back garden. I sat enjoying the silence, watching the bees darting around the honeysuckle bushes, weaving in and out of the flowerbed. It didn't take long for the headache to fade away. I had worried when I'd decided I wouldn't return to work after my accident, that I would be bored. That I would find the weeks until the baby arrived endless and lonely, as I had in the hospital. Instead though, there was a deep sense of peace and contentment to my days. I had been taking long walks along the river every morning. I had been gardening, pruning and planting, loving the closeness with nature.

There was just one thorn among my garden of roses and that was my little sister. She still, after almost five months, had not come back home. She was never far from my thoughts. Where was she? Why hadn't she at least called to find out if I was okay? If Isabel was right, Bonnie had freaked out because she thought I was going to die. Why hadn't she come back to comfort Isabel and Lucas? Why hadn't she come back to say her goodbyes, attend my funeral? Was she really such a coward? I knew why she was scared to face up to reality, but I couldn't stop myself resenting her selfish behaviour. I couldn't believe that she would abandon us all at such a tough time. She knew, more than most, how scared I was about this pregnancy. She knew Isabel would take on more than she should and would need her to step in. But still, she stayed away. I hoped when I saw her – if I saw her – again, that I would be able to find the strength to forgive her. To put aside my hurt and anger and accept her back into my life. But a small part of me wondered if I would have the strength to do it.

The sun was getting high now, and I decided to head back in and clean the bath. I needed to be doing something. I felt suddenly filled with energy, as if I could move mountains. As I stood up from the wooden bench, I heard a tiny pop. My eyes widened as I felt warm liquid trickle steadily down my legs, soaking my jeans. My waters had broken. I stood, awestruck and unmoving for a minute, digesting what this meant. My son was on his way. I was going to have my baby. And then, before I had even taken a step towards the house, a contraction rippled through my belly.

I had dreamed and imagined what this would feel like for so long. I'd read countless books, watched videos on YouTube, but this feeling, this powerful sensation was nothing like I had imagined it would be. I could feel every single muscle tightening in my abdomen. It took my breath away. A few seconds later, it was over, and I wondered if I had imagined the whole thing.

I rushed inside, stripping off my wet jeans and pants, throwing them into the washing machine. I realised my t-shirt was damp too, and pulled it off. I stood naked in the kitchen, wondering what I should do. Another contraction came then, and I smiled in relief and amazement. It was real. It was happening. When the contraction ended I had the sudden thought I should call someone. I should call Lucas. But I didn't want to. I had started this pregnancy alone. Just me and the baby, wondering, wishing and waiting to see if he would make it. It had been a special, extraordinary secret of my very own. The start of something deeply bonding, almost magically so, between the two of us. And now I realised I wanted it to end the same way. Me and my son. Just the two of us, our special, sacred birthing experience. I didn't feel fear. I didn't feel uncertainty. I felt absolutely powerful and I knew I could do this.

The contractions were coming fast. The midwife had told me they might take some time to build up, hours or possibly even a few days, but this was no hesitant experience. They quickly increased, coming every few minutes, lasting longer and longer. I walked through the house, gripping the furniture for support as they grew stronger, rocking my hips, feeling the baby moving lower and lower. It was more intense now. When they came, I couldn't think of anything else. I was entirely in the moment, lost in the sensation, my only goal was to breathe, to get through it.

Now there was no abstract sense to each contraction. There had never been anything more real, more visceral than this. My fingernails clawed deep grooves into the soft wood of the banister as another one washed over me. A low animal moan rippled from my throat as I twisted my hips to and fro, feeling a pressure with the power of an erupting volcano build within my body. I found myself so caught up in the intensity, the agony, that I couldn't picture it being over. There was just pain, pure overwhelming pain. I was tearing in half. I was going to explode. I couldn't take it. Tears streamed unrestrained and barely noticed down my cheeks, and I flung my head back in desperation, unable to take any more of this nightmare. But then, as quickly as it had started, it ended again. I looked up amazed to find myself in my own home, alive and well, the dizzying spasms over, though I knew my moment of rest would not last for long.

I moved into the living room, grasping the mantelpiece for support, groaning as I felt another one ripple through me. I felt as though I was walking through fire, my body burning. Other times it was like being pulled in two different directions, tearing through the centre. Despite my discomfort, every single one of the epic surges made me happy, knowing it was bringing me closer to meeting my child. I felt more human, more alive than I had ever known.

The next contraction sent me falling to my hands and knees. Something was happening. I could feel my body pushing. It was the most intense feeling I had ever experienced, it was as if I was turning inside out, ripping in two. I was losing all semblance of control now, my body had overruled my mind, and there was nothing but sensation, instinct, surrender. Roaring screams came unbidden from my lungs, I had no way of stopping the sounds, any more than I could stop the powerful pressure of my baby pushing his way into the world. I knew this was the point where I was at my most vulnerable. I needed to trust that this was what was supposed to happen, but it was just so strong. It frightened me. Suddenly I realised the importance of this moment, the million things that could go wrong. I was overwhelmed. It wasn't what I thought it would be, it was so much more. The power I had felt earlier was replaced by fear, uncertainty and I wished that I wasn't alone.

But then, with a scream that shook the foundations of the house, I could feel the head crowning, pushing unstoppably through me. I looked between my legs and saw a round little head hanging there. It was surreal and beautiful and terrifying all at once. I panted, catching my breath, feeling utterly shell shocked at what had just happened. With my hands and knees on the rug in the living room, I realised with absolute clarity that with the next contraction, my life would be changed forever. I was about to become someone else. The thought gave me the strength to continue. I *would* do this. I had no choice but to do this. I ran my index finger over the base of his neck, checking the cord wasn't wrapped around him. It wasn't. I moved into a squat, grabbing a cushion from the sofa and placing it between my legs. Then my body took over once again, and in one fierce, bellowing push, he slid from my body, landing in a tangle of limbs on the white cushion, staining it forever with his beautiful arrival.

For a few seconds nothing happened. I just stared at him. He was pink and wrinkled, his hair fluffy and auburn, just like my sisters'. He blinked. He opened his mouth. And then he let out a startling cry, shocking me into action. Sinking down onto the floor, I scooped the wriggling bundle up into my arms, bringing him to my naked chest. He was so small, so soft. I could feel his heart beating beneath my palm. He was absolutely real, and he was perfect. He stopped crying, his body curving to fit mine, his tiny fingers grasping onto my breast, though he didn't suckle. He breathed in deeply, closed his eyes and drifted off to sleep, and I couldn't help but giggle at the absurdity of it. As I stared at my son, my own child, my beautiful baby, one thought swam through my mind over and over again.

I am a mother. I am a mother. I am a mother.

Five minutes later I still hadn't moved. The cord dangled from between my legs, snaking it's way up my abdomen and finishing at the baby's navel. I didn't want to move yet. I couldn't. I felt dizzy and tired and weak. I looked at the clock on the mantelpiece and was surprised to see it read five thirty. Had I really been in labour so long? Lucas would be back from work at any minute, I should do something to clean up, make us look less shocking, I thought, looking at the stained cushion, the streaks of dried blood running down my thighs, across my arms. But, as I heard the key in the lock, I realised it was too late. It didn't really matter anyway. I remained completely still as the front door opened and closed again.

"Roxy, I'm home," came Lucas's rumbling voice. "And I brought muffins!" He stepped into the living room and stopped dead in his tracks as he saw me. One hand went to the door frame as if to steady himself. He dropped the bag he was carrying onto the carpet. It landed with a soft thud.

"Surprise," I whispered. "He's here."

Lucas shook his head, his eyes wide. "You didn't call."

"No." I felt queasy, my hands shaky, my body shuddering, but I managed a smile. "I'm glad you're here now. Come and meet your son."

Lucas stepped forward tentatively. He looked beyond shocked. Then he seemed to come to his senses. He grabbed the thick crocheted blanket from the back of the sofa, and crouched down, wrapping it snugly around me and the baby. "You're shaking."

"It's been a strenuous afternoon."

"You should have called." He leaned in, running his finger over the baby's head. "Roxy, he's perfect."

I nodded. "I know."

"Is he okay? Are you okay?"

"Yes. I think so." A pain rippled through my abdomen and my face creased.

"What is it? What's wrong?"

"Just... just the placenta. Get a bowl."

He stared at me for a second, then rushed into the kitchen. He was back a moment later with a big mixing bowl in his hands. "What should I do?" he asked, his eyes glittering with fear. I took the bowl in one hand, careful not to disturb the baby sleeping in my arms.

"Nothing, you don't need to do anything." I squatted over the bowl and a moment later the placenta dropped into it. Lucas's eyes were wide.

"Is that... is it over?"

"I think so."

"What now?"

I grinned up at him. "Now, you help me to bed."

Thirty minutes later after Lucas had helped me wash and dress in clean pyjamas, I was sipping a hot cup of tea and eating my way through an enormous chocolate muffin. Lucas sat on the edge of the bed, holding our son, grinning from ear to ear. I'd stopped shaking, and now felt a sense of absolute bliss and contentment. "So what are we going to call him?" Lucas murmured, running his fingers over the silky smooth skin of the baby's rosy cheek.

"Oscar. I think he's an Oscar," I replied, stifling a yawn.

"Oscar," Lucas repeated. "Oscar Bowen. We've waited a very long time to meet you little one." He kissed his cheek and then placed the baby on my chest, covering the pair of us with the warm duvet. I felt like someone completely different. Someone who understood new levels of happiness, previously uncharted depths of emotion. As Lucas climbed onto the bed and settled his arm around me, I felt like I would burst with love for him too. The way he was looking at me made me certain he felt the same. "You are the most incredible woman," he murmured softly into my ear. "I'm in awe of what you just did. But tell me," he asked, his chocolate brown eyes burning into my own, "did you always plan to do this alone? I know we didn't talk about it, but I assumed you would want to go to the hospital?"

I shook my head. "I didn't want to go anywhere. I don't know... I didn't plan it, but when my waters broke, I knew I didn't want to do anything to disturb it. He was coming, and I knew I could do it. I was so sure."

"You were right."

"It was amazing, Lucas. So amazing. There were points where I thought I couldn't cope anymore, but I just kept reaching further and further. I realised how much I'm capable of. Honestly it was the best thing I have ever done. I'm sorry I didn't include you in it. I thought you might be scared."

"I would have been. I don't want to lose you. I want to keep you safe. But I would have respected your choice." He kissed the top of my head.

"I know you would have," I replied sleepily. I felt Oscar shuffling around, his lips smacking together against me. Smiling, I unbuttoned my pyjama top and offered him my breast. He latched hungrily, and I felt tears spring to my eyes.

"Does it hurt?" Lucas asked, concerned.

I shook my head. "No, it's just... I never thought I would be here. Doing this. I've waited so long for this moment."

"Me too."

"I want it to last forever."

"You deserve so much happiness, Roxy. We all do. Everything has changed for us now. This is a whole new chapter of our lives." He eased his arm out from behind me, lowering my head onto the pillow. I moved Oscar so he was lying in the crook of my arm, still feeding ravenously. We watched him, his perfect rosy cheeks, his tiny moon shaped fingernails, his little button nose. I had done it. I had kept him safe and now he was here. I was finally a mother to a living, whole, beautiful boy, and I planned to be the best mother he could ever wish for.

Chapter Fifteen

I was in heaven. Raw, unrefined heaven. My pillows were butter-soft beneath my head, the smell of the fresh damp air streaming through the open window, cooling and awakening. The downy pink bundle in the crook of my arm lay completely still, his mouth wide, his eyes glued closed. Every now and then I would dip my head, hovering my ear just above his face to check he was still breathing, so at peace in his slumber it was impossible to tell.

Somewhere around day two I had started to believe it was real. This baby was mine. I had made him, I had carried him and now I had birthed him. I was really a mother. In truth, though I had always been too embarrassed to voice my feelings, I had considered myself a mother from that very first pregnancy. Something had changed from that moment, and though I had never got to meet or hold them or discover all the wonderful intricacies of the tiny beings that would have become my children, I had loved them all the same, unconditionally, keeping a space for each of them deep within my heart. But I had never talked of them. I had never referred to myself as a parent. It would have brought up too many unanswerable questions, too many painful memories. Oscar had changed that for me. I stroked my finger over his silky smooth cheek, wondering how long he would sleep. Soft footsteps sounded on the stairs and I looked up to see Lucas entering the room, bringing a tray of tea and buttered crumpets.

"You don't have to do that. I *can* get up you know?" I laughed.

"Don't you dare." He put the tray down on the bed beside me and leaned over to kiss me, resting his forehead against mine. "You've earned a long rest in bed. Enjoy it."

I smiled. Lucas was loving his new role as a doting father. He'd insisted on calling the midwife to check me and the baby over after the birth, and after she had given us the all clear, he had relaxed noticeably. I'd barely left the bed in the three days since Oscar had arrived, not due to exhaustion or illness, but because Lucas had insisted I savour these precious early days, and honestly I was far too content to argue with him. I'd waited too long for this to want to rush it. Oscar and I had been getting to know each other over the previous few days, and I had fallen deeper and deeper in love with him as every minute passed. He was a relaxed, happy little thing, he slept a lot, fed frequently and cried rarely. In fact, the only time I ever heard him complain was when I changed his clothes. He didn't like to be manoeuvred and manipulated into a new vest, and protested loudly, his face turning almost as red as his hair.

Lucas picked up the camera from the bedside table and snapped a photo of Oscar and I. A knock at the front door echoed through the house. "I bet I can guess who that is," I smiled.

"She's been calling non-stop. I told her it was okay to come today," Lucas said.

"Well go on then, don't leave her standing around on the doorstep."

"Spoil sport." He grinned and disappeared out of the room. A minute later Isabel poked her beautiful face around the door.

"Hey," she whispered softly.

"Hey you."

She tiptoed in, coming to sit beside me on the bed. "Oh my goodness... he's gorgeous. Roxy, you're a mummy. You have an actual baby!"

"I know."

"It suits you. You look absolutely radiant."

"I thought the radiant part was supposed to come during the pregnancy, not after?" I giggled.

"Well, when have you ever followed the rules, hey? Can I hold him?" she asked, looking longingly at Oscar. I nodded, though passing him over was more difficult than I had anticipated. The moment his warmth left my arms I felt an overwhelming urge to snatch him back. I resisted somehow, contenting myself with sitting beside Isabel and watching his peaceful little face.

"I wish Bonnie was here too. I can't believe she's missed so much. She doesn't even know she has a nephew," I murmured. Isabel looked at me and I saw something unreadable in her eyes. "What?"

She shook her head. "It's probably not the right time..."

"What is it, Issy? Tell me."

She sighed, looking down at the baby. "Well, I

suppose there's never a good time, is there? It's Bon. She wrote to me, I just got the letter a few days ago."

"What did she say? Is she alright?"

"See for yourself." She balanced Oscar on one arm and reached into her brown leather handbag. Fishing around inside it she pulled out a crumpled envelope, disconcertingly slim. She handed it to me and I took it with shaking hands, sliding the letter out carefully.

Isabel, Roxy,

I know I should have been in touch sooner. I'm so sorry. I didn't stop caring, it was just such a massive shock, Rox, seeing you like that. I was scared. I think you'll understand why. I read every single report in the news, and I was so relieved to see that you were okay.

I just don't feel ready to come back yet. I'm not ready to resume my life. I just need some time. I know you probably think I'm being selfish, but there are things you can't understand, things I can't put into words for a letter. It's complicated.

I will come back. I just need time.

I love you both so much,

Bonnie xxx

I read the letter in silence, my fingertips pressing into the thin paper as if I could reach my sister through the fine sheet. I could feel Isabel watching me, concern etched on her features. "Well," I spoke finally. "I'm glad she's alive. I just wish she had given us a way to get in touch with her. I don't like that she's going through whatever it is she's struggling with on her own."

"We don't know that she's alone. She could be with friends."

"Perhaps." I looked at the letter again, turning it over, hoping to see an address or a phone number.

There was nothing. "She sounds pretty clear headed. Like she understands what she needs. I guess we just have to be patient. Wait for her to come home."

"I think that's all we can do. It's what she wants."

"I know. I can't tell you how relieved I am to hear she's alright." I felt a surge of happiness, a weight lifting from my shoulders. I couldn't feel angry at Bonnie for not staying. I couldn't judge her for running away. She had her own problems, her own issues she needed to work through, and I couldn't resent her for putting herself first for a change. Knowing that she was out there, living, resting, whatever it was she was doing, even if it was in less than ideal circumstances, made me feel light and happy. "This is a very good week," I smiled.

Isabel nodded, putting her hand on my cheek. "It is. I have a feeling things are going to get better and better from here, Rox. For all of us."

Chapter Sixteen

Five months later.

"Hi baby, we're home!" I called, pushing my way through the back door and into the kitchen. I dropped the heavy bags full of fresh food onto the kitchen table and stripped off my coat and scarf, sweating in the heated house after the frigid air outside. Oscar was fast asleep on my chest, cocooned in a sling, and I could already see his face glowing rosy red. Leaving the shopping on the table, I padded upstairs. I could hear the shower running.

"I'll be out in a minute," Lucas called. "You've been ages!" I popped my head through the door as the shower shut off. Lucas was drying himself with a massive fluffy towel.

"I know, time got away from me. I went to the Saturday farmer's market after I met the girls, I've got loads of stuff."

"Food?"

"Yep. I probably should have taken the car

though, it was a bloody long walk with all those bags, and this little monkey is getting heavy. And he threw up his milk all down my chest. I had to give myself a wipe down with baby-wipes!"

"Yuk. Is he okay?"

"Just indigestion I think. I'm going to put him down in bed, he's making me boil." Lucas nodded, following me through to the bedroom and pulling on a pair of jeans. The day had been blissful so far. I'd met up with a couple of friends from work for brunch, both of them mothers too, and we had chatted about nappies and feeding, bedtime routines and how none of us ever had time to wash our hair anymore. The kind of topics that should have been mind-numbing, but were actually indescribably fulfilling. I loved it. All of it. I loved meeting other mums for coffee while our babies rolled on the floor or slept in our arms. I loved waking up at dawn, snuggling together in bed before taking a stroll outside, Oscar on my hip as we listened to the sounds of the birds waking up.

Every day was similar, yet never predictable. He was doing new things every week, smiling, babbling, getting little chubby thigh rolls. He was teething now too which was an added challenge, but I had nothing but sympathy for him. Even when he was screaming I found myself almost looking down from above, smiling at the image of us swaying on the carpet wearing holes in it, blissfully aware of how lucky I was to have him at all. It was so much more than I had ever hoped for – I even tackled the baby singing groups with a smile on my face.

I unstrapped the sling and lowered the sleeping baby onto the mattress, where he rolled on his side and nuzzled into a blanket. I smiled. He was a miracle to me, and watching him sleep was one of the best parts of my day.

"Do you want to go to the park when he wakes up? Or the soft play maybe?" Lucas asked, keeping his voice low so as not to wake Oscar.

I stood up, stripping off my jumper, and was hit with a dizzying wave of head rush. A splitting pain bolted between my eyes and my vision clouded, Lucas's face blurring. I tried to say something, to answer his question, but I couldn't seem to summon the words. A crashing, whooshing sound rang in my ears, deafening me and I lost all sense of up and down, my balance slipping away. I realised, with a strange sort of detachment, that I was falling. My head was exploding. Blackness was engulfing me.

I opened my eyes, to find myself laying in Lucas's lap, my head cradled in his arm, his deep dark eyes panicked and concerned. I could see all the details of his face. The thunder in my ears had gone entirely. I felt fine, if a little confused. "What happened?" I asked, staring up at my husband.

"That's what I was going to ask," he said. "You fainted. I only just managed to catch you before you hit the floor. How do you feel?"

I pulled myself up to a sitting position, assessing the situation. "Actually, I feel fine."

He shook his head. "You must have exhausted yourself going out for so long, carrying all the shopping back. You aren't getting enough rest as it is what with all the night-time feeding and Oscar's teething. You need to take it easy," he insisted, brushing the hair back from my face and tucking it behind my ear.

"I was. I am. I don't know what that was, I just

came over all dizzy. I must have stood up too fast after putting Oscar down. And it's too hot in here."

Lucas frowned. "Head rush? You think it's normal to faint because of a head rush?"

"Maybe. It could be hormones. My body's all weird at the moment, it's adapting. I'm sure it's not uncommon for a new mum to have a fainting spell."

Lucas nodded, still frowning. "Perhaps. But whatever the reason, you need to rest."

"I'm not tired."

He was already pulling back the duvet, guiding me into the bed. "Lucas!" I protested. "I still need to put the shopping away. And it's the middle of the day, I don't want to go to bed."

He ignored me, pulling off my jeans and t-shirt, leaving me sitting on the mattress in my underwear. "Rest. Sleep. You need to take care of yourself." Oscar was beginning to stir and Lucas scooped him up. "Hey little one. What do you say us boys go for an adventure?" Oscar gave a gummy smile and grabbed for Lucas's nose, and I couldn't help but grin.

"You're being over the top," I said, though I knew him well enough that I was sure he wouldn't back down.

"I'm making sure you don't burn out." He kissed me softly, his breath warm on my skin, then lowered my head down onto the pillow. He offered Oscar's tiny little cheek for me to kiss too. "We'll be fine. Won't we Osccy?"

"Don't call him Osccy!"

"Rest." He blew a kiss and left, leaving me feeling utterly lost. What would I do now? It had been a long time since I hadn't had Oscar to keep me busy. As I lay between the cool cotton sheets, listening to the sounds of Lucas banging around in the kitchen putting the shopping away, then opening the front door and heading outside with my son, I felt suddenly heavy. I *was* tired. I hadn't really thought about it until now, but Lucas was right. I felt it deep within me, an undercurrent of absolute exhaustion. Reflecting on how well my husband knew me, I let my eyes close. I would sleep. And I would not think about the fact that I had just lied to him. I would shut away that thought, block it out, so it wouldn't be true.

Chapter Seventeen

Two months later.

I glanced anxiously at the clock, then back to the beautiful baby suckling at my breast. I would be late if he didn't finish his feed soon. Stroking a finger across the downy silk of his chubby cheek, I wondered how the time had passed so quickly. How could he be seven months old already? The time leading up until his birth had seemed as if it were stuck in tar, each second lasting a lifetime as I'd waited nervously for him to come. Yet the moment he was born, everything had changed. Now life was on fast forward and I found myself grabbing desperately to the moments, holding onto them tightly. It was all going too fast.

Oscar's eyes sank closed as he released my nipple, his mouth open wide as his head lolled back in a deep, satisfied sleep. Gently, I eased myself off the sofa and carried him through to the kitchen where Lucas was sipping an espresso. The rich smell I had once loved so much still sent waves of nausea through me. Pregnancy had ended a lifelong love affair with coffee, and I still couldn't bear the slightest whiff of it. I swallowed, holding back the urge to vomit, and Lucas looked up.

"Sorry, angel," he said, jumping up from the barstool and opening the window to let the aroma dissipate. "Is he done?"

"He is. Fast asleep and full to burst." I deposited the sleeping bundle into Lucas's arms and kissed him once more on his rosy cheek. I couldn't ever seem to kiss him enough, I always needed just one more. "There's expressed milk in the freezer if you need it, but I should think I'll be back before his next feed anyway."

"Okay," Lucas nodded, his big bear like hands cocooning Oscar, who nuzzled into his chest. "Are you sure you don't want us to come with you? I don't feel right about you going alone. That's why I took the day off."

"No, no," I shook my head, picking up my bag from the counter, throwing my phone inside it. There was a bundle of screwed up tissues curled up within the deceptively chic leather, covered in dried, milky sick. I pulled them out with my thumb and index finger, tossing them in the bin and sniffing the inside of the bag. It was still passable. I looked up at Lucas. "I don't want Oscar having his nap disturbed, and the hospital will be full of germs. It's better that he stays here. It's just a quick scan, I'm sure nothing will come of it."

He nodded uncertainly. "If you're sure. But call me the moment you get out, okay?"

"I will."

He leaned forward, careful not to disturb the baby, and kissed me softly. I breathed in the smell of my husband, wishing I could just spend the afternoon cuddled up with the two of them rather than trekking across town to go to a stupid hospital appointment. Finally I pulled back. "I'll see you soon," I said, looping the strap of my bag across my chest. I stole one last kiss from Oscar and then I turned and left before I could change my mind.

This is pointless. This is such a waste of time. I wonder what it's costing the NHS? It's like being buried alive. I want to get out! The thoughts played on a loop as I endured the MRI scan, the thundering machine moving and adjusting around me. "Just try to relax, Roxanne," a voice called from somewhere nearby. "It's nearly over." I bloody hoped so.

After I'd managed to convince Lucas not to call an ambulance after a second "collapsing incident," he'd insisted that I, at the very least pay a visit to my GP. To keep the peace, I had agreed, explaining to my poor overworked doctor that I was so sorry for taking up her time and that I was sure it was just a case of exhaustion after a particularly rough patch of teething.

Oscar had been sleeping in twenty minute bouts and I would just be falling asleep when he began crying again. It was like some sort of inhumane torture, but a rite of passage I was undeniably proud to be going through. Yes, I'd had bad headaches and dizzy spells which I had tried to keep hidden from Lucas, and I craved my bed more often than not, but that was what it meant to be a mother. I certainly didn't need a doctor.

To my surprise and annoyance, Dr. Laken had

asked me in great detail about the car crash, and had fixated on the fact that I had suffered a concussion. She'd insisted on booking me in for an MRI scan and follow up appointment at the local hospital, and no amount of arguing on my part had swayed her into changing her mind. I'd been put out by her interference. Fed up with the whole situation I had lied to Lucas, telling him she'd agreed with me that it was just lack of sleep causing the dizzy spells. And he'd believed me – why wouldn't he? – that is, until he'd opened a letter from the hospital inviting me for a brain scan.

And so here I was, wasting a perfectly good afternoon being subjected to a claustrophobic nightmare. *And it smells like coffee in here.* A deep voice rang in my ears. "Okay, Roxanne, we're all done. Just give us a moment and we'll have you out of there." The machine whirred and then I was squinting uncomfortably as the florescent lights came into view above me.

"You okay?" the radiologist asked, holding out a hand for me to grab, helping me to stand up.

"Yes, I think so," I nodded. "So, what's the

verdict?"

"I'm going to assess the images now and pass them onto the consultant neurologist. Then we'll let you know."

"Oh, okay," I said, clutching the flimsy gown around my body uncomfortably, wondering why they made them so sheer. I kept my back pressed against the table to prevent it from flapping open. The radiologist kept his eyes firmly on my face and I was thankful for his discretion. "So do I go home now?"

"Oh no, it won't take long. Get dressed and then Kate will show you where you can wait," he nodded towards his assistant and she smiled. "You can grab a coffee and someone will be through to see you shortly."

"Mrs Bowen?" A tall woman in a pretty blue dress was standing in the doorway. Her brown hair was twisted in a neat knot at the base of her head, and reading glasses hung from a thin thread around her neck. "I'm Dr Reed. Would you follow me?" I grabbed my bag and shoved my phone back inside it as I followed her out of the waiting room and down a long empty hallway. I'd been trying to call home, but there was no signal in this part of the hospital. It would have to wait.

We entered a sparse room with a large desk in the middle. "Please take a seat," Dr Reed said, closing the door behind her.

"Thank you." I sat down suddenly nervous. I wiped my palms discreetly against my dress. "So, am I dying?" I joked, wishing immediately that I could take the words back. "Sorry, that was insensitive," I shook my head. "I'm sure you have to break bad news all the time. It must be hard."

I didn't miss the flash of discomfort that coloured her expression. "Yes," she nodded cautiously. "I'm afraid I do." She leaned forward across her desk and I suddenly had an urge to get up and run.

"Mrs Bowen... Roxanne." I chewed my lip, leaning back in my chair. My foot began to tap involuntarily, the uneven rhythm pounding against the tiled floor. Why was she looking at me like that? *I should go... I need to go.* The doctor continued. "I've been looking at your scan pictures and I'm afraid we found something... of concern."

The room became very still. I could hear the clock ticking on the desk, footsteps far away at the end of that long eerie hall. I could hear my own breath.

"What is it?" I whispered, suddenly terrified.

"A tumour," she said simply. "We don't know if it was triggered by your head injury during the car crash, but it is a possibility. Mrs Bowen, there are many types of brain tumour. The one you have is known as a Glioblastoma." She paused, her eyes sliding uncomfortable from my face. "I'm sorry to say it's a grade four tumour."

"What does that mean? Can you get rid of it?"

She shook her head. "Some tumours, even some Glioblastoma can be operated on. However, yours is in a very deep location within the brain. The way these tumours work is to grow outwards like a vine, wrapping around the tissues, suffocating them..." she shook her head again. "Roxanne there's no easy way to say this, but honestly, I'm amazed you're still functioning at all. The tumour you have is one of the biggest I have seen. It is completely inoperable. It's compressing several vital areas of your brain, and most worrying of all, it's pushing up against the brain stem. If it grows much larger, which I suspect it will – and quickly – your respiratory system will be affected."

"Affected?"

"It will shut down," she said bluntly. "With the type and size of tumour you have we would normally give patients six to twelve months. I would suggest yours is close to a year old."

"Six to twelve months of what?" I asked, my brain fuzzy with confusion. My ears were ringing, and I rubbed them with the heels of my hands, trying to focus on her words.

"Life. Six to twelve months of life. The crash was," she looked at her notes, "almost a year ago."

I let her words sink in. Did it mean what I thought it did? "How long do I have left?" I whispered.

"I don't know for certain. Weeks. Maybe a month or two. Not long I'm afraid, Roxanne. You must have been in a lot of pain?" she asked, raising an eyebrow. "Terrible headaches. Dizziness. Vomiting? Why didn't you come in sooner?"

I blinked silently. She was right. The headaches had been almost unbearable at times, like I'd thrown my skull into a brick wall. And though I never spoke of it, I was often dizzy. But I hadn't wanted to say anything, to ruin my time with my son. I'd waited so long for him, I wasn't going to waste it complaining.

Oscar. My baby. How could this be happening? How could she be telling me that I was going to die, and soon? My body felt as though it was crumbling in on itself, my head sinking to my knees, my hands covering my face. Fear and panic coursed through my veins. I didn't know what to do. "What should I do," I whispered, more to myself than to her. "How do I stop this?" I raised my eyes to her, pleading for a miracle.

"I'm sorry, Mrs Bowen. I know this has got to be a big shock for you. We will of course give you something for the pain. You don't have to endure the headaches any longer."

"What about chemo? Radiation therapy or whatever it's called? There has to be something!"

"We can go down that path, if it's what you choose. But I must warn you that this type of tumour is notoriously resistant to treatment. There are a few other options we can look at, but it's important that I be realistic with you. My professional opinion is that anything we do at this stage would buy you a matter of weeks at most, at a very high cost. I will give you all the information you need to read through, and you can make an informed decision over the coming days." She looked at me, then shook her head, turning away. "I'm truly sorry, I know that it's not what you wanted to hear."

I sat, dumbstruck, unable to reply, unable to formulate my thoughts into anything that made sense. Was this woman, this *specialist* really saying sorry to me? What a pitiful word. What a pointless sentiment. Sorry. Sorry that you're going to die and leave your baby – the baby you've waited years for – without a mother to raise him? Sorry that after all you've been through, you still can't enjoy peace, happiness. *Fucking sorry?* What a waste of breath.

"Mrs Bowen," she continued, "there is counselling available. To help you, you know, process all of this information. You're not alone in this. Would you like me to refer you?"

I met her concerned gaze, my eyes cold and hard. Fury unlike anything I had ever felt before flooded my body, making my hands shake. "Counselling?" I whispered. "Counselling?" I stood up, pushing back my chair, leaning forward, my hands slamming down on her desk. "Fucking counselling!" I yelled, swiping the lamp from the shiny maple surface and hearing a satisfying crunch as it shattered on the tile. "You want me to sit and talk about my feelings, is that right? Well, let me tell you how I fucking feel shall I? I didn't do anything to deserve this! None of this. For five years, I've said goodbye to my babies over and over again. I lost a part of myself with every single one that left me, every face I never got to see. Do you understand how that feels? Can you even comprehend how much that hurts, a mother of five with no babies to hold, no children to love? It tears you apart."

"Mrs Bowen, please sit down," Dr Reed said softly, gesturing to the chair.

"And then," I continued, ignoring her instruction, "I get told I'm having a son. A healthy, strong, beautiful baby boy. But do I get to enjoy it? No. Of course I don't. I get hit by a fucking truck, nearly died myself. Nearly lost him. But I didn't though, did I? I made it. And *he* made it. And now he's here and he's the best thing in my life, the only thing I ever wanted and I love him so much that sometimes I can't even breathe with the intensity of it. I would do anything for him. I finally have everything." I kicked the desk, not caring that I was causing a scene.

"I'm not wishing for the world, just to be a mother, to raise my son, to see him grow. But I can't even have that, can I? What did I do!" I screamed. "Why?!" I picked up a half filled glass of water, intending to throw it against the wall, consumed with rage.

"Roxanne! Stop!" Dr Reed commanded. "Please, just calm down, let's talk about this. Please, take a breath."

I paused, sneering at her. I took a breath, exaggerating the movement, heaving my chest in and out. "Well, isn't that a surprise?" I said, my voice dripping with sarcasm. "I took a breath, and yet look, here we still are. And I'm still dying. And nothing has changed. Nothing!" I bellowed, smashing the glass into the desk. Blood splattered from my clenched fist as the glass sliced through my skin. It burned and I could tell that it had cut deep, but it didn't matter. I could just bleed to death right now and it wouldn't matter.

My eyes filled with tears. "Why can't I just be happy? Why can't I keep him?" I whispered, my voice barely audible. The tears splashed heavily down my cheeks and I wiped them with my palm, smelling the sharp tang of metal and sweat. "I wanted this so much," I whispered. "It wasn't enough."

Dr Reed watched me silently, her eyes cautious, one hand gripping the telephone receiver. Her knuckles were white and for a brief moment I felt guilty. She wasn't to blame. She was just the messenger. But I couldn't find a way to apologise. The words wouldn't come. And I wasn't sorry. Not really. I was too numb for anything other than the bitterness of my fury. I turned for the door, and without a backwards glance, walked through it leaving a trail of blood and broken glass in my wake. Ten steps down the corridor I heard the unmistakable sound of my doctor bursting into tears.

Chapter Eighteen

I don't know how long I'd been in the hospital, but when I emerged from its prison like confines I found that the bright sunshine had been replaced with a raging storm. I stood blood soaked and howling in the rain, before falling to my knees. The patients, visitors, even the doctors passed me by, fearful of this crazed woman, unwilling to be drawn into my pain. I saw a mother pull her child back from me, steering him through the door to safety. Lucky her. Getting to make that choice. Getting to be his mother. Lucky fucking her.

I walked home through the rain, the words *"completely inoperable"* ringing over and over again in my mind. How had I survived this long? How could I have ignored it for so long? Would it have made a difference if I hadn't? Perhaps my fate had been written the moment I got in my car to buy apple pie all those months back. The front door was unlocked and I pushed it open, listening for the sound of my son. My husband.

"Rox, is that you back?" Lucas called from the living room. I didn't answer. Instead I slumped against the front door, feeling it slam closed as my legs gave out from under me. I slid down the door, sitting on the welcome mat, unable to go any further into the home that would no longer be mine.

"Rox?" I heard him get up. I couldn't move. "Did you get soaked. That storm came out of nowhere!" he exclaimed, stepping into the hall. His eyes travelled down to where I crouched, sopping wet and utterly filthy. The colour drained from his cheeks. "Oh my god! Oh bloody hell, Roxy what happened?"

He rushed toward me, kneeling down in front of me. "Oh god, you're covered in blood. Were you mugged, darling?" he asked, wiping my face with his sleeve, pushing my matted hair out of my eyes.

I shook my head. "Not mugged. Robbed."

He frowned, taking my tear-stained face in his big, warm hands. "Roxy, what do you mean?" I shook my head, unable to speak. He stroked my matted hair then leaned back. "Come on." He pulled me up and I leaned heavily against him. I didn't want to walk. "Darling come on, we need to clean you up." He took my hand and suddenly realised where the blood was coming from. "Shit!"

I yanked it back. "It's fine."

"No it bloody isn't, it's practically down to the bone. You need stitches. What the hell has happened to you, Roxy?" he demanded.

"I don't need stitches. There's no point." I walked past him into the kitchen and turned the tap on, running the water over the wound, ignoring the searing pain that radiated in sickening waves through my palm. I could feel him watching me, unsure what to do next. I looked up at him, hating myself for having to say the words, but unable to hold them back. I had to tell him. "She said I'm going to die, Lucas. I should be dead already." Tears sprang to my eyes and I did nothing to hold them back.

"What are you talking about?" Lucas whispered, stepping forward. His hands went to my face and I sank into his touch.

"The scan... She said I have a tumour. A grade four tumour. She said it's one of the biggest she's ever seen, and... and... they can't do anything to get rid of it. Lucas, she said I'm going to die soon. It's going to stop me breathing and it could be as little as a few weeks," I whispered, barely audible over the sound of the running water.

"No," he breathed.

I nodded. "Yes."

"No!" he said fiercely. "No!" this isn't going to happen, they got it wrong. No fucking way, Roxy, you're not going anywhere." He pulled me into his arms, holding me tightly. I wished I could stay there forever.

"I'm sorry Lucas, I'm so sorry."

"Don't be. You aren't going anywhere. You just aren't." I heard his voice crack and his chest heave in silent sobs as he pressed his face against my hair. "You aren't leaving us," he told me through broken gasps.

Then why are you crying? I thought bitterly.

Lucas bandaged my hand, washed my face and helped me change into a dry dress. Then he placed a steaming cup of tea in front of me. I felt numb. Completely empty. It was as if I had died already. What was the point of continuing now?

"We're going to fix this, Rox," he was saying.

"How? How are we going to fix this Lucas? They don't have an operation for fixing this, it's too deep, it's spread out like a spider stretching across my brain." I shuddered at the image.

"There is so much happening in medical science now, Rox. There will be options. We're getting a second opinion. We're going to make this better, I promise." A cry sounded from the living room and our eyes met with the unspoken words we dared not speak aloud. That if I died, Oscar would have to grow up without me. Motherless. I couldn't stand the guilt, yet I could do nothing to change it. Lucas stood, and a moment later I heard him cooing to our son. "Did you have nice dreams?" he asked softly. He came back through and placed the baby in my arms.

Instinctively, I positioned him at my breast, watching as he latched onto my nipple, his chubby hand rubbing soft circles as he kneaded at my chest. Everything about him was perfect. I couldn't leave him. I couldn't.

I held him tightly, rocking gently from side to side. He pulled back, burped and smiled up at me, one lonely tooth poking out of soft pink gums. I sat him up and he gurgled, leaning his forehead against mine as he often did. And I suddenly realised I couldn't do it anymore. It wasn't fair. I wasn't going to get to be his mother. Lucas would have to be everything he needed from now on. I wasn't going to be the one who got to feed him. I wouldn't get to cuddle him to sleep or wake up to his sing song voice as he grabbed for his toes. I wouldn't be there for his first steps, his first word, his first anything. I was leaving and there was nothing I could do to change that. Without a word, I stood and placed him in Lucas's arms.

"Roxy, what are you doing?" he asked, his eyes bloodshot and rimmed with red.

"I'm so sorry Lucas," I said, bending forward and kissing him on the mouth. "I have to go. I can't pretend to be his mother, your wife. I'm none of those things now. I'm nothing anymore," I said, my voice wobbling.

"Roxy, don't be ridiculous. Put your bag down, you're not thinking straight."

"I can't. I can't stay knowing I'll have to go soon. I can't let him need me like this when I can't promise to be here. It's not fair." I closed my eyes and kissed my son's dewy lips. Goodbye, my darling," I whispered, my voice cracking.

"Roxy..."

"Goodbye, Lucas. I love you. I'm so sorry I can't stay with you both." And before he could stop me, I was walking away, leaving behind everything that mattered to me. His voice echoed behind me down the street, but I didn't slow. I had nothing left to give them now.

Chapter Nineteen

Darkness had fallen as I'd been walking. The rain slashed cold against my face, stinging my eyes and burning my cheeks raw, but I didn't care. My thighs burned with the exertion of my escape and I shivered against the cold, but I pushed forward. I had to keep going, though I had no idea where to. I had nowhere to go now. I walked blindly, the roads twisting and turning, following my feet, not caring where I ended up. I had no idea what time it was but as I rounded a corner I realised it must be late. There were people here, dressed to party. A row of seedy clubs lined the pavement and the crowds outside were laughing, dancing, their merriment sickening.

I turned from them, walking through the dark open doorway into the atrium of the first club on the strip. It was hot and dry, and I squeezed the rain from my hair, watching it pool on the sticky floor. My dress was soaked through and no amount of wringing out was going to rescue it. Wiping the moisture from my face I followed the thumping beat into the throbbing womb of the club. The music was deafening, bodies twisting and gyrating against one another on the dance floor. Walking around the edge of the chaos, I found what I was looking for. I elbowed my way through the crowd, reaching the bar.

A man barely out of boyhood, with floppy brown hair and a diamond stud in his ear, moved to stand beside me, shouting something inaudible over the music. I shrugged, frowning and he imitated drinking, pointing to the bar. I nodded and he called something to the barman, handing over a crisp note. The barman put a shot of something clear down on the slick surface in front of me and I lifted the glass to my lips, smelling the spicy, acrid contents. I threw it back in one mouthful, the heat of the alcohol travelling through me, putting a stop to my convulsive shivering. The floppy haired man-child was patting me on the back, saying something, smiling, but I was already manoeuvring through the crowd, walking away from him, ignoring his shouts of protest.

I pushed my way into the sea of bodies, marvelling at how simple things were for these people. How they could dance and laugh, when my world had ended. I wondered if any of them realised how precious their lives were. How free they were. How much possibility lie ahead of every single one of them. I envied them. I hated them. But I hated myself more.

I emerged on the opposite side of the dance floor, bursting free of the writhing bodies, propelling my way out of the throng. I needed space. Fewer people were mingling over this side, and I walked towards a dark, secluded archway, stepping through into a small alcove. A few tables were dotted around. Empty. The music was quieter here, and I rubbed my temples, hating the pain in my head, willing it to do it's job and kill me now. What was the point in waiting? Where was the mercy in making me live with this triggered bomb ready to detonate inside me, scattering my brain to pieces at any moment?

An abandoned bottle of beer stood on a table nearby, and I walked towards it, picking it up and bringing it to my lips. A hand reached out of the darkness, wrapping itself around my wrist before I could take a sip. I gave a start, my eyes travelling along the thick muscular arm, meeting deep blue eyes shining out from the darkness. Not empty. Not abandoned. The stranger stared at me, his mouth twisted in a questioning smile, and I felt an energy buzzing in the space between us. The promise of escape. Obliteration.

Standing, he stepped towards me, his eyes still locked on mine, his hand not leaving my wrist. He plucked the bottle from my hand, taking a swig before holding it to my mouth. I let him pour the cool, fizzing liquid onto my tongue, swallowing thickly. Wordlessly, he put the bottle back on the table, then took a step closer. I didn't move away as he closed the space between our bodies. He grabbed my other wrist, glancing only briefly at the blood seeping through the crisp white bandages my husband had lovingly wrapped earlier. Holding both of my wrists against my chest, he began walking me backwards until I felt the wall, hard against my spine.

For a brief moment, I felt a cold wave of terror. *I shouldn't be here. I should leave.* But I didn't move. His twinkling eyes fixed on mine. He lowered his head, his lips inches from my own, his breath on my skin, seeping through my parted lips, warming somehow. He sank lower, and I didn't stop him as he kissed me, hot and rough and fierce. It was so different from what I was used to I almost pulled away. But I couldn't. I wouldn't, because in that moment he was the only thing standing in the way of my empty, meaningless reality, and I needed it. I needed him.

His fingers ran down my throat, unbuttoning my dress and slipping inside the wet cotton, grazing against my bra as his tongue slipped deeper into my mouth. Beer and cigarettes. Different.

His hand slipped beneath my bra, cupping my breast.

It doesn't matter.

His other reached beneath my skirt, fingertips running up my thigh, pushing aside my underwear.

It doesn't matter.

His breath was on my neck. I felt the hardness of him pushing against me and I knew I should stop him, but still I said nothing. I wanted him to keep going. I wanted to feel him push inside me, to have him fill the gaping, hollow darkness that had consumed me completely. I felt as though I had been opened up, scooped out and discarded. I couldn't stand it. He paused for a second, pulling back a little, his eyes on mine as if to ask, "Is this okay?"

This was my chance to say no. *No it's not okay. I'm a wife, I'm a mother. Of course it's not okay!* Only I was none of those things now. Roxanne Bowen was dead. I was just the empty shell that was left. So I said nothing. Instead, I lifted my foot, placing it flat against the wall, spreading my knees wide as I opened myself to him. And then, it was too late. His lips found my throat, and he was thrusting into me, hard and full and fast. And I was right. It was exactly what I needed. I rocked my hips, taking him deeper, letting myself be carried away. But it was different. It was too different. He smelled all wrong, our bodies didn't mesh like they should. He wasn't Lucas.

I can't do this.

He ground his body against mine, and rather than the pleasure I needed, the distraction to numb my pain, the emptiness inside me was growing somehow, bigger than before, threatening to swallow me up from the inside out.

What am I doing?

His body pushed against mine and I could smell the cheap aftershave on his neck.

I can't bear it.

His hands came to my bottom, lifting me higher, grunting as he slid deeper.

I have to stop him.

He freed my breast, his tongue circling my nipple, teeth grazing against my skin. My mind flew to Oscar, suckling softly, seeking the warm milk I had made just for him and I felt a spasm of utter repulsion at what I was doing.

I have to get him out of me!

Suddenly I was screaming and thrashing, pushing against him. I swiped my nails across his cheek and saw blood well up, three long wounds marking his skin. Stunned, he stumbled back, hands up in surrender, cock still swinging from side to side. Disgusted, I pushed past him, yanking my dress down, fumbling with my buttons. Back through the ocean of sweating, throbbing bodies. They groped and grabbed, rubbing against me as I passed, calling to me. I hated them all. I needed to get out. I needed air. I couldn't stand it! Finally I broke through the double doors, past the cackling girls and burly bouncers, and I ran. I ran as if I could escape myself, but no matter how hard I tried, I couldn't seem to get away.

Chapter Twenty

About a mile from the club, I could run no more. My legs gave out and I fell to my knees, the hard wet tarmac sending tremors of pain through my bones. I wiped a wet, gravel smeared hand across my forehead, sweeping my hair back from my face before vomiting the entire contents of my stomach onto the pavement. I paused for a minute, breathing hard, before climbing up onto shaky legs, bracing myself against a lamppost.

What am I doing? What did I just do? That wasn't me. I don't know who that woman was, but it wasn't me! Tears were streaming down my face and I wiped the wet fabric of my dress ineffectively across my cheeks, looking around at my surroundings. I felt utterly lost. Where had I run to? I didn't recognise a thing. I had no idea where I was, and I didn't care. I didn't want to be found anyway.

Across the road, the bright lights of a Tesco superstore shone welcomingly in the darkness. I walked blindly towards it, feeling a burst of determination. I stepped through the automatic doors, head down, relieved to find that nobody tried to greet me. Here, I was anonymous. I liked that.

My body seemed to know what I was looking for before my brain caught up. My legs carried me towards the alcohol aisle. Row upon row of neat, colourful bottles. Wine... beer. And the spirits. My fingers wrapped around the neck of a bottle and I smiled as the weight of it swung into my hand. Jack Daniels. I had never been a whisky drinker. I'd always preferred gin, or wine. But in this moment, the thick glass bottle was what I needed more than anything else.

Cradling it to my chest I quickly paid, not waiting for my change. I held the bottle tightly, as if afraid someone might take it from me, heading for the door and walking back outside into the darkness. The streets were quiet now, a fine drizzle misting the air, chilling me to the bone. I walked with purpose looking at signs, following a well trodden route down to the river. I stumbled down the sloped grassy verge, the mud sliding beneath my feet, and continued along the tree lined tow path.

The moon was barely visible behind the thick clouds, and the path was unlit. I reflected how I would usually be terrified walking in such a vulnerable situation. Any other day I wouldn't dream of being so reckless. But this wasn't any other day. If I slipped and fell, it wouldn't make a difference. If those looming shadows the trees and bushes were casting across the path turned out to be a serial killer, I would simply thank him for speeding up my departure.

It wasn't that I was fearless. No, in fact I felt a constant pulsing terror at what was coming, what I was leaving behind. But beyond the fear, there was one presiding element. Coating me, sheltering me within it's cold clammy grasp. Numbness. I was sure it must be a self protective measure. If I remained numb, I wouldn't have to face the reality. If I was numb, I could avoid the burning, unfiltered agony simmering just beneath the surface.

I steered my way a little off the path, heading for a tall, thick trunked tree and sinking to the ground beneath it. I could still see the ripples of the dark water a few metres away. It was comforting. I spun the lid off the heavy bottle, bringing it to my nose, and sniffing deeply.

The smell was enough to drag me back into a never-ending stream of memories. I closed my eyes, letting myself be transported to another place and time, picturing my mother, my beautiful Rosie, dancing in the kitchen with a glass half full of Jack. She would throw her long ginger hair back over her shoulder, drink deeply, cough and then laugh. It was before she got too ill to be fun, but after she stopped being the mum I had always known. A strange middle ground, where she was more open than she had ever been. A time when we would talk and talk and talk. When she wanted to hear my secrets, and I still trusted her enough to share them with her. I sniffed the whisky again, picturing her soft smiling face, the way she would take me in her arms when I was upset, telling me there was only one me. That I was irreplaceable, and precious and how I had changed everything for the better for her. God, I needed her now. I needed my mother to hold me tight and make everything okay again. I needed her to do the things that mums do to fix their children's problems.

I had gone through my whole adult life without

her. I'd never let myself need her, not when I'd married Lucas and neither of my parents had been there to see it. Not when I lost my five tiny babies and felt like the world was swallowing me up. Not when I'd had the most incredible experience of my life, pushed myself further than I realised I could ever go by giving birth to my son. Not ever. But I did now. I needed her desperately. I needed to be taken care of, loved, fixed. I was so sick of being broken. My body had failed me time and time again, and now it was taking everything I'd worked for, everything I cared about.

I took a swig of the spicy whisky, relishing the discomfort as it burned a trail down my throat, wiping my mouth with the back of my hand. It was getting colder and I pulled my wet clothes tighter around me, my teeth clashing together as I shivered. A high pitched jingle sounded, and I realised it was coming from my bag. My phone. Fishing it out, I looked at the display, the words unfocused. Squinting, I made out Lucas's name. I stared at it for a few moments, knowing I wouldn't answer. Finally the ringing ceased and the screen lit up. Sixteen missed calls. Most of them from Lucas, some from Isabel. There were messages too. Texts and voicemail. I didn't click to open either. Instead, I summoned all my strength and launched the phone into the river, listening as it splashed into the dark murky waters.

My thoughts went to Oscar. Was he sleeping? Did Lucas have enough milk for him in the freezer? Was he crying for me? I forced myself to shut out the image. I couldn't let myself think about it. I couldn't do anything to stop what was going to happen. It didn't matter that every single part of me wanted to go home, to pick up my son and never put him down. The choice was no longer mine to make. And there was no point lamenting how unfair it was. It just *was*.

I leaned back against the tree, holding the bottle like a baby, my fingers running up and down the cool glass, sobs rumbling raggedly through my chest. I shouldn't have thought of him. I shouldn't have opened myself up to this pain. I craved the numbness again. I craved oblivion. But it was too late, Oscar was all I could see, smell, feel. I wanted him with me. I wanted him more than I could stand. His face burned brightly in my mind, tauntingly cruel. I curled my legs tighter against my body, letting my head rest against the tree, gasping for breath as the sobs intensified, and hoping to the universe that I would die in my sleep. I didn't want to see another sunrise if I couldn't have my child.

Chapter Twenty-One

I woke with a start, jumping to my feet, dashing forward in confusion, my soles colliding with the hard wet earth. My foot looped beneath a tree root and I catapulted over it, slamming hard into the ground, gasping for air. My mouth was coated with mud and grit and I spat it out, feeling a bruise already blooming on my cheekbone. Shaking and scared I pushed myself up on my elbows, realising how close I'd come to running straight into the river. Awareness seeping slowly back to me, I remembered where I was, what I was doing out here all alone. The clouds had dissipated a little, the rain had departed at last, and the moon shone down brightly, still high in the sky. I couldn't have been asleep for more than a few hours.

I pulled myself up onto my feet, rubbing my hands up and down my arms, feeling like I would certainly crack a bone if I continued to shiver so furiously. I was ice cold, every single muscle in my body aching and torn. I tasted blood and realised I must have bitten through the side of my cheek as I slept.

Gingerly I ran my tongue over the chewed flesh, wincing. The glint of the whisky bottle in the grass caught my attention and I moved to pick it up, unscrewing the lid and bringing it halfway to my lips before suddenly changing my mind. I shouldn't drink when I was so dangerously cold. If I took even a swig of the whisky now, my blood would be pulled to my extremities, quickly cooling before travelling back to my vital organs, lowering my core temperature significantly.

The life saving memory had popped into my head just in time. The advice had been shared with me by the medic during my first and only anthropological expedition, when I'd travelled to Tanzania. It had been right at the end of our trip, our work all done and the whole team had been about to hike Mount Kilimanjaro just for the challenge of it. He'd told us that two women had got stuck in a bitter snow storm on the mountain the previous year, and only one had made it back down for this very reason. It was no joke. Drinking alcohol could kill me in this state. But then again, given my situation, perhaps it wasn't such a bad idea.

I stared at the bottle, deliberating, wondering why I didn't just do it. I couldn't seem to summon the courage. I craved heat. Roaring fires, scalding hot tea, hot water bottles. I wanted to be wrapped in warm arms, held until my body thawed. I stamped my feet, flinching at the pain in my half numb toes. I had to get moving. I had to walk. Tossing the bottle back on the grass and turning my back on it, I jogged up the path, back into the deserted street above it. I headed for the street lights, uneasy in the darkness, unsure where to go. I still had my bag, my purse. Perhaps a hotel? I could've called a taxi if I hadn't thrown my bloody phone in the canal, I thought, grimacing at the hazy memory.

I didn't want to walk. Every instinct in me wanted to curl up and go back to sleep, but I couldn't. I had to keep going. My mind fought against my body, forcing it to keep putting one foot in front of the other. There was a Hilton near town, though I had no idea where town was in relation to me. But they would have a twenty-four hour reception. They would have cosy, warm rooms... thick blankets. Of course, given that I looked like a tramp who had just lost a street fight, I wasn't altogether certain they would give one to me, but I couldn't worry about that now. I'd deal with that if and when I found it.

I crossed the road, heading in what I hoped was the right direction. My legs were shaking but I ignored the desperate urge to stop. I had to push forwards. I *had* to. As I rounded a corner I saw a couple, a man and a woman I guessed to be in their early twenties, walking hand in hand about fifty feet ahead of me. They strolled slowly, heads inclined towards one another in intimate conversation, though I couldn't hear their words. I felt a sharp stab of jealousy as I was dragged back to a memory of the early days with Lucas, when he and I would walk home from a party, our hands clasped tightly together, much too in love to rush. We'd been so happy back then. My chest tightened, but I shook the emotions off, focusing my attention on the pair ahead of me.

"Hey!" I shouted, beginning to approach them at a run, ignoring the pain in my calves and the stabbing in my half numb feet. They turned, startled and I noticed how the man stepped in front of the woman, his stance protective. Her hands wrapped tightly around his forearm, her eyes wary.

"Hey!" I repeated, breathless. "Can you tell me where I am? I'm trying to get... to the Hilton." I stopped in front of them, bending forwards, my hands on my thighs as I tried to catch my breath.

The man regarded me coolly. "*You're* trying to get to the Hilton?" he repeated, his tone incredulous.

I nodded. "Yes, I am. Am I anywhere near it?" I asked, noticing the waver in my voice as I swallowed back a fresh wave of tears. How there could be a single drop left to cry I couldn't fathom.

The pair looked at each other, the woman shaking her head. "The only Hilton I know of is about six miles north of here. Near the football stadium. Is that the one you mean?"

"Six miles?" I gasped. I could not walk another six miles. I couldn't. I doubted I'd even manage one.

"Yeah." The woman looked at me, stepping past her boyfriend. "You're soaked. And bleeding," she frowned. "What happened to you?"

I shook my head, the tears welling up in my eyes now. "It's... it's b-been a rough day."

"Can I call someone for you?" she asked, touching my arm. "Fuck, you're freezing!" she startled as her hand met my skin. "Here." She took off her jacket, wrapping it around my shoulders. It was thick, woollen and smelled like perfume. I was shocked at the gesture.

"Oh no, please – " I started to protest, moving to slip the coat back off.

"Don't you dare." She buttoned it around me, her eyes on mine. "You need this more than I do right now."

"Thank you," I whispered.

"Was there a reason you needed to be at the Hilton?" the man chimed in now. "Because if it's just a hotel you're after, there's a Travelodge about five minutes from here."

"Really?"

"Yes, really."

"Can you tell me how to get there?"

He shook his head. "I don't think so." He looked at the woman, sharing some sort of unspoken communication, the kind that came from having a deep foundation of intimacy. I watched silently, soaking up the warmth from the borrowed jacket. He turned back to me after a few seconds. "We'll go with you. I wouldn't feel comfortable leaving you to walk there all alone in the state you're in... uh, no offence, I mean – it's late. Let us come."

The woman nodded alongside him. "It's not far, we would really prefer it."

I meant to protest, to decline their kind offer, but I was just too exhausted to be polite. I didn't want to get lost. All I wanted was a warm bed somewhere quiet where I could curl up and rest. With their help, I could be there in minutes. I nodded, humbled by their generosity. "Thank you. That's kind of you."

We walked in silence mostly, the woman's arm on mine, occasionally supporting my weight when I stumbled. Even with her help, I could barely find the strength to keep going. I was grateful that neither of them asked any further questions. I couldn't have formed the words to answer them even if they had.

As the Travelodge came in to view I found my strength again, my steps quickening in my desperation to get inside. We stopped on the pavement in front of the entrance and I began to unbutton the coat.

"No, you keep it," the woman said.

I shook my head. "I'm not going to let you walk home without a coat after all you've done for me." I handed it to her, trying to hide the fact that my body was protesting against the frigid air on my skin once more. I began to shake, my teeth chattering together. "It will be warm in there," I reassured her, nodding towards the building.

"Okay, well get inside then. Do you want us to come in with you?"

"No. Thanks, but I'll be okay from here. I really appreciate you showing me the way."

"It was no trouble," the man replied. "Now go, get warm okay?"

I nodded, offering them a small smile. "Thank you both." I walked into the bright foyer of the hotel. A blast of heat above the door hit me and I stopped beneath it, reluctant to leave the delicious warmth.

"Can I help you?" a sharp voice called, and I looked to where it was coming from. A woman, grey haired and hard mouthed was staring at me from the welcome desk.

"Yes," I said, dragging myself away from the hot

spot and walking towards her. "I need a room please."

"A room?"

"Yes, whatever you have available."

She regarded me, unsmiling. "You know this isn't a dosshouse?"

I stared back, my expression hard. After the day I'd just had, my patience was all but gone. I was freezing cold, hurt and exhausted beyond belief. And I wasn't going to let this woman treat me like dirt, no matter how I might look to her. "A room," I repeated, my tone cold. I pulled my purse from my bag, slapped my credit card on the desk and folded my arms. For a moment, she did nothing, deciding, I assumed, whether or not she should refuse me. Though I didn't allow my hard expression to slip I felt absolutely terrified at the thought that she might send me back out into the cold. I was so close, so very close to getting a bed. She was my final hurdle and I couldn't afford to fall now.

With a loud tut, she picked up the card, slid it into the reader and told me to enter my pin. Her eyes flashed in surprise when the transaction went through. Without a word, she handed it back to me, along with a white plastic key card. "Room 127. Just so you know, any damages or theft will get charged to your card." She glared at me. I didn't have the energy to come back with a clever retort. I had the key. I had what I needed. I turned, walking away, and pressed the button for the lift which thankfully arrived within seconds. I could feel her watching me as the doors slid closed, but I didn't look back. I didn't care what she thought of me.

I emerged into a long, quiet hallway, the carpet soft beneath my feet, the lights blissfully dim. Swiping the card, I entered my room, shutting the door firmly behind me. She had given me a twin room, two single beds separated by a small bedside cabinet. I didn't care. I stripped off my wet clothes, hanging them on the heated towel rail in the bathroom. Then, in a burst of hurry, I pulled the thick duvet from one bed and dumped it onto the other. Flinging open the wardrobe I found four thick fleecy blankets. I added two to the bed and wrapped the others snugly around my naked body. Then I climbed onto the mattress, crawling beneath the mound of covers, curling into myself. Very slowly I felt the convulsive shivers subsiding. My eyes closed, and I couldn't find the strength to open them again.

Chapter Twenty-Two

There was a shrill ringing sound shocking me into consciousness, assaulting my fragile senses. I jumped out of bed, staring wildly around, wondering where it was coming from. The telephone on the bedside cabinet flashed purple with each sound and I picked it up, if only to make the ringing stop. My head spun, my vision black around the edges, dizzying head-rush intermingled with a sharp slicing pain in my temples. I sank back down onto the bed, burrowing under the covers, holding the receiver to my ear.

"Roxy... are you there?" came a deep, familiar voice.

"Lucas..." I breathed, his voice pulling something lose within my chest. "H-how did you find me?"

"Credit card." *Of course. Shit.* "Roxy, stay where you are, I'm coming to you."

"What? Lucas, no, please don't!"

"We'll argue in person, okay? Now just tell me what room you're in." I shook my head, trying to alleviate the pain. "Roxy?"

"It's 127." I slammed the phone down, my eyes watering as I buried my face in the pillow. Being awake hurt too much, I wanted to sleep. It was all I could think of. A quiet voice in the back of my mind told me I should leave, get up, get dressed and go. Lucas was going to come and I didn't have the strength for that conversation. But right now, I didn't have the strength for anything. I pulled my legs to my chest, and didn't fight the exhaustion as I let it drag me back to unconsciousness.

I didn't know how much time had passed, but it was long enough for me to fall back into a deep sleep. When the knocking came I woke suddenly, pulled from a nightmare I was grateful to have escaped. A baby had been crying, locked behind the thick rusted bars of a bare cell, his eyes bloodshot and pleading as he screamed for me, pulling himself up to stand against the walls of his cot which stood lonely in the centre of the filthy prison cell. I'd thrown myself against the bars, numb to the bruises and injuries as they mounted up. I didn't care, I just needed to get to the child. But the bars wouldn't budge. Nobody came to help me, though I screamed until my lungs burned.

The baby's cries grew desperate and I shook with maternal instinct. The need to pick him up, to comfort him consumed me as it crawled beneath my skin. Then suddenly, though I hadn't believed anything could be worse than the crying, the baby went mute. I could no longer see his face, though I knew he was still there, hidden beneath the blankets. The silence was terrifying. He was fading away. And I still couldn't get to him. I was screaming and fighting but it made no difference. I knew that I couldn't save him, it was hopeless, but I also knew that I would keep trying until my last breath.

I lay against the hotel pillow, breathing hard, covered in sweat, wondering if I'd been shouting in my sleep. The knock sounded again, more insistent this time. With slow, careful movements, I stood, eager to avoid another sickening bout of head-rush. Wrapping a blanket around myself I stumbled to the door, swinging it back on its hinges. There on the threshold stood my husband, dishevelled in a creased white t-shirt and old blue jeans. The jeans he only wore when he was sick. Comfort jeans. Our eyes met briefly, and I looked down at the carpet, unable to say a word. "Oh, Rox..." he breathed. He stepped forward, wrapping his arms around me and I let him, melting into his chest, too tired to fight.

He pushed the door closed and led me back to the bed, sitting down beside me and taking my hand. I threw a quick glance at him, drinking him in. I had really believed that I would never see him again. I could smell his skin, warm, a little damp from the rain. He smelled alive. Real. But none of this felt real to me. How could it be? Me sitting here in this bleak little room, no more than a stranger to the man I had vowed to spend my life with. How could he even begin to understand, to accept what was happening to me, when I no longer recognised the person staring back at me from the mirror? Who had I become in the hours that had followed that hideous scan?

I wanted to go back to this time yesterday morning. I wanted to cancel my hospital appointment and stay at home with Lucas and Oscar instead. Sing to my son. Feed him to sleep. Then make love with Lucas on the rug in the living room, whispering conspiratorially, giggling like teenagers as we tried not to disturb the slumbering baby. I wanted my headaches to disappear, the dizziness to become some distant memory. I wanted to stay.

Lucas's thumb ran lightly across the back of my knuckles and I jerked away, folding my hands in my lap. My fingernails dug into my palm as I shook the tidal wave of emotions off. "Where's Oscar?" I croaked, realising he'd come alone. "Lucas, where is he?"

"It's okay, don't panic. He's at home. Isabel's with him."

I nodded, though I didn't feel comfortable knowing Oscar was alone with Issy. Would she know how to care for him? Had Lucas shown her what to do? "Is he... how is he?"

Lucas shook his head. "He's heartbroken, Rox. He's not used to being without his mummy. You know I'm only second rate, you're the favourite. He's been screaming half the night and he won't take a bottle."

"What? He has to, he needs the milk. Fuck, Lucas! Has Issy tried feeding him instead of you?"

"She's trying now. But it's not the same, he needs

you, Roxy. He needs his mother."

I sank back, leaning against the pillows, my chest tightening painfully. "He's going to have to learn to live without me. You both are." My voice didn't betray the pain in my heart at the thought of my son crying for me. My palms began to sweat, twitching as I pushed aside the overwhelming instinct to go to him.

Lucas's shoulders slumped. He looked at me, his eyes soft and glistening. He moved closer, though he didn't take my hand again. For a long time he said nothing. Then finally he spoke, his voice hoarse. "Maybe. Maybe we will have to learn to let you go. But not yet." His deep brown eyes burned into mine and I met them defiantly, refusing to let him see how close I was to crumbling. "Roxy, you're acting like you've already died. You're not being fair – on any of us, least of all yourself."

"It's going to happen, Lucas."

"But you don't know when! It could be months, years even. What are you going to do, just waste the time you have left waiting to die, living in some kind of limbo when you could be savouring the last precious moments with us? With the child you wanted so much?"

His words hit me like a ton of bricks. My fist went to my mouth as if I could push the hurt away, my knuckles scraping roughly against my lips. Was I being selfish? I'd thought I was doing what was best for them, walking away, making a clean break before Oscar got too attached. But that was bullshit, wasn't it? He was seven months old and I was his world. There was no question that he was completely and utterly attached to me. Did it make it any easier if I walked away now? Or was it just easier for me? To walk out of my life, cut my ties because the alternative was something I didn't have the courage for? How could I stay, hold my son, feed him, fall asleep between him and Lucas, knowing I couldn't keep them no matter how much I wanted to? How could I force Lucas to live with the knowledge that one day he was going to come home and find me dead? How could I bear it?

"It's not fair," I whispered, my hand trailing down the bed, linking my fingers through his, squeezing tightly. "It's just not."

"No." He lifted my hand, kissing my knuckles. "But it's not fair that you cut us off like this either. We want you back, Rox. We want you right until the end, whenever that may be."

"How? How can it possibly work? You can't leave me alone with Oscar, I could drop dead at any moment, and if you're at work – he'd be alone with me, all alone!" I cried, my voice rising in panic at the thought of it.

"I won't leave you. We have enough savings to manage for a while, I'm going to take some time off and then when you're feeling more settled, I might go back part time and get a helper in to stay with you. I'll ask my parents maybe. You won't be alone, darling."

"If I come back, I won't have the strength to leave again. It was hard enough the first time."

"Good. I don't want you to ever do that again. Have you any idea how scared we've been, Rox? I had no idea where you'd gone, what might have happened to you."

I looked away, guilty as I pictured the stranger in the club the previous night. What *did* happen to me? What would happen to me if I kept wandering? I knew the answer to that. I would do everything I could to speed up my departure. I wasn't brave enough to do it outright, but that didn't mean I couldn't cause myself some serious harm if it meant not living with the uncertainty of my future. I would drink until I numbed the pain. I would forget to eat. I would search out other ways to harm myself, forget who I was and why I was running from my life. Maybe I would even put aside how awful I had felt about myself last night, and once again let a stranger do what he pleased to me, if it meant taking me away from my reality for a little while. I would commit a slow, cowardly, painful suicide that my family would read about in the news. And that was the most selfish thing I could imagine doing to them.

They deserved better. I knew it now. I knew that Lucas was right. I needed to go home. I needed to be the wife I had promised to be, until death do us part. I needed to hold my son until he was dragged from my arms, give him all the love he deserved while I still could. I needed to leave them with a memory of me that was worth something. I needed to create my legacy. "Okay," I nodded, looking up at my husband who was watching me closely. "Okay. I'll come home with you."

Chapter Twenty-Three

Something strange happens when you realise you're going to die. Not just realise, actually. Accept. When you accept today really could be it. This could be the last sunrise. The last smile. The last kiss. Suddenly, everything comes into focus. Every minute becomes a gift.

It took four days after Lucas brought me home. He ran me a bath, then tucked me in bed placing Oscar in my arms, and I'd cried until I couldn't breathe. I'd felt like my insides had been torn out. I'd wanted it to be over, right then, that very moment. I couldn't bear the waiting.

But then something changed. Acceptance. I guess I'd passed through the five stages of grief, though I still don't know what they all are. Is having sex with strangers in clubs and nearly freezing yourself to death on that list? Maybe. All I knew was that one morning I woke up to the sound of Lucas in the shower, Oscar sleeping peacefully beside me, and I wasn't afraid anymore. I understood that nothing I said or did or wished would make the slightest bit of difference. And I knew, with blinding clarity, that I was wasting time.

I climbed out of bed and padded softly into the en-suite, leaving the door ajar so I could hear if Oscar cried for me. Pulling off my thick fleecy socks and baggy t-shirt, I threw them on the tile and peeked around the shower curtain. Lucas jumped when he saw me, his hand flying dramatically to his chest. "Jesus, Rox, you nearly gave me a heart attack!"

"Sorry," I smiled, my eyes travelling down his broad, soapy shoulders, his wide, strong chest. I stepped into the shower, arching toward the warm flowing water.

"Is... uh, is everything okay?" he murmured.

"You tell me." I leaned forward, kissing him deeply, pushing my body against his. When was the last time I had done this? I couldn't even remember.

"Oh," he said as I pulled back a little to look at him. "Oh." And then he seemed to remember how this dance went. His hands slid down my waist, his lips found mine and he pushed me against the cold wall, taking me, reclaiming me. I did not count it as wasted time.

"I want to go kayaking," I told him through a mouthful of bacon and buttery bread. I'd decided there was little point in sticking to sugar free muesli now, I may as well eat what I pleased.

"Kayaking? Why?"

"I've never done it. I found this place in Dorset where you can hire them. It's a pretty calm stretch of water. We can even take Oscar."

"Hmm. Yeah, maybe sometime," he answered absently.

"I want to go today," I told him, taking a deep glug of tea.

"Today? Uh, I dunno, Rox. Shouldn't you be resting or something? Shouldn't we go and see the consultant at hospital?"

"No." I'd already decided I would not be setting a foot back in that hospital. Not until they wheeled me in on a stretcher and deposited me in a fridge, in any case. There was no point. The consultant had told me everything I needed to know, and unless there was some medical breakthrough in the immediate future, there was nothing else they could offer me.

I stood up, sweeping the crumbs off the counter and onto my plate with the side of my hand, before dropping it into the sink. I didn't bother to wash it. "I'll get Oscar's bag ready. And the camera," I added as an afterthought. It would be nice for them to have some photos of our adventure to look back on. The calmness I felt took me by surprise. A few days ago the idea of taking pictures to remember me by would have thrown me into despair. Acceptance, I realised again.

"Finish your food and we'll meet you in the car, okay?"

Lucas was staring open mouthed at me. "Rox..."

"Five minutes," I ordered, picking up the changing bag and walking out of the room before he could argue with me. I threw nappies and babygrows into Oscar's bag. A warm blanket, a few books. Then impulsively I pulled a suitcase out from under the bed, tossing a jumble of clothes from Lucas's wardrobe into it. I opened my own wardrobe and grabbed a handful of items, throwing them on top of the pile. Then underwear, toiletries, my journal. I jammed the case shut and grinned at Oscar who was lying on his play-mat, kicking his legs in the air. "You ready, angel?" I whispered, excitement bubbling in my belly.

"What's this?" Lucas asked as I clattered down the stairs, baby under one arm, the heavy suitcase bumping along beside me.

"Clothes. Things we might need."

"For kayaking? For a day trip?"

"It might be longer than a day. There are a few other... adventures I want to try."

"Rox... I'm not sure I want to do this. It doesn't feel right. You're supposed to be ill. Recuperating. We can't just go away."

"Lucas," I breathed, plopping Oscar down on the carpet. "Darling." I put my hands on his cheeks, pulling his face down to meet mine, touching my forehead to his. "There isn't going to be a recuperation. You know that."

He shook his head, his eyes wet. "We have to try."

"It won't help."

"It might."

"It won't."

"You expect me just to go along with this? To just give up? Stop trying? You expect me to just let you go? I can't do it, Roxy!" He pulled away from me, his eyes wild, desperate. I moved towards him again, closing the gap between us, wrapping my arms around him and resting my head on his chest, the sound of his heart thrumming in my ear. I had always fit perfectly against his body, my head always positioned right beside his heart. "It only makes that sound for you," he had once told me.

"I wish it was different," I whispered. "I wish I could give you me. I wish we were going to grow old together, just like I promised we would," I swallowed. "But I don't have any of that to give now. All I have to give you is this time, this moment, right now. And if I'm lucky, the next, and the one after that. I don't know how many moments I have left, but they're yours. All the time I have, it's yours."

I felt him kiss the top of my head, and turned to wipe my tear-streaked face against his t-shirt. "Lucas," I murmured into his chest. "It's all I've got. Time. Memories. Let's make it mean something, okay? Let's not waste it wishing for the impossible." I pulled back, looking him in the eye.

He stared at me in silence for a long while, so long I began to think he might refuse me. Then he leaned forward and kissed me slowly, as if he could kiss away all my pain. Finally he pulled back. "Okay," he said, his voice gravelly. "Let's make some fucking memories."

Chapter Twenty-Four

There's nothing worse than enforced fun. The grand kayaking adventure had turned out to be an absolute disaster. The sunshine had disappeared behind thick ominous clouds, the air turning bitterly cold around us as we donned our life-jackets. Oscar had begun bellowing the moment we stepped off dry land, into the shaky, unstable contraption. I was sure he could sense his safety was no longer the secure thing he had counted on just moments before. We'd pushed on, in spite of all the signs, all the warnings, both Lucas and I pasting wide, fake grins onto our faces, pretending it was all part of some massive adventure, hollow laughs ringing in our throats, not daring to break the brittle scene with any slip from character. Meanwhile, we had continued to ignore the fact that I knew Lucas wanted to talk about my impending doom, and I resolutely did not. We'd formed some sort of unspoken agreement, a deal that we would play nice, have the time of our lives, live for the moment, even though the reality was pure shit.

Hot air ballooning, the second of our epic adventurous activities had turned out to be a similarly disastrous affair. I was fast discovering that ticking items off a bucket list wasn't nearly the cathartic, exhilarating experience I had hoped it would be. Perhaps creating memories in this artificial way was the wrong way to go about it. In the end, I knew, Lucas would remember the obscure things about our time together. The smell of my skin in the morning. The look in my eye when I had said, "I do." The way I always finished his pudding at restaurants, or that time I had worn my new court shoes on the wet decking outside our favourite bar, and had slipped over knocking a waiter carrying a tray full of drinks flat on his back. The silly things. The first times. The arguments and the make ups. I knew he would remember these things, because they were the kind of memories that played on my mind now about him. The first time we held hands. The way he always brought me strong tea and a blueberry muffin in bed on the anniversary of my mother's death, though he never said why, or even mentioned the date. The little things that meant far more than any bucket list adventure.

Yet Oscar would have none of these memories of me, us, our life as a family. He would have no happy times to look back on, no idea of how much I had loved him. He deserved to know, and over the course of our trip I had come to a decision on what I needed to do, how I would preserve my love for him. I just hadn't had the courage to do it yet. I'd put it off, scared to face it. But now I felt a pull that I couldn't ignore. The time had come to be brave.

We were staying in a cosy little cottage on the coast of Devon, having travelled all over the West Country for almost three weeks. I was sitting at the bay window in the bedroom, scrunched up with my legs beneath me in a low chesterfield armchair, a patchwork quilt wrapped loosely around my shoulders. My feet tingled painfully and I shifted my position to let the blood flow into them, noticing that at last the sun had begun to emerge in weak rays from the horizon. Another long, empty night had passed, and though I had spent the first four or five hours in bed, cuddled up with Lucas and Oscar, I'd given up on any hope of my own slumber as the clock had ticked the hours away. Finally, and inevitably as was always the case, I had come to sit, watching the stars and listening to the quiet contented breathing of the two people I loved most in the world.

I'd been waiting, trying not to think of what I had to do, how I could face the truth of my situation, how my fear was of no consequence, because the task was too important for my discomfort to impede it. I wouldn't let my son down, I wouldn't leave him with nothing to hold on to. Now as the first streams of daylight began to filter into the warm, peaceful room, Oscar began to stir right on cue. I went to him, scooping him up out of the big bed before his fidgeting woke Lucas, and carried him through to the low beamed living room. A fire, one I had tended on and off throughout the night, was glowing softly, warming the room. Standing in front of the sofa was a tripod, my new video-camera attached to the top, fearsome in its silent expectation. Pressing the little red record button, I took a deep breath and moved to sit down on the faded blue sofa in front of it, placing Oscar on my lap. I looked down at his sweet little face and felt utter terror at what I had to do. I wanted to run. To escape my fate and bury my head in the sand forever, but Oscar deserved so much more from me, and I knew now, my path was set no matter what I did.

"Oscar," I began, my voice wobbling as I looked up at the lens of the camera. "My darling boy. I don't think there's a child on this earth who is more wanted or loved than you are. You have been a dream, my only dream, my only wish for so long. I spent years missing you before I even knew who you were. Actually, I sometimes worried that I was building motherhood up to be this mystical unobtainable thing that would change me, change the whole world around me. I worried my expectations were too high," I laughed, dipping my head down to kiss my son on top of his soft downy head. "I was wrong. You surpassed my expectations beyond anything I could have imagined."

My eyes met the earnest gaze of my son and I felt a jolt of emotion so strong I thought I would break in two. How could I say goodbye when I had barely had chance to say hello? How could I face the truth that I would leave him motherless and there was nothing I could do to stop it? "I wish..." I shook my head, searching for the right words. "I wish I could see what you look like as you watch this, sweetheart. How you've changed into a big boy, a teenager, a man. I wish I could be there by your side through it all, my darling," my voice cracked.

No! No. This wasn't the right way to do it. This weepy message of despair was not how I was going to leave my child. I stood up and stopped the recording. I would not leave him the farewell of a desperate, broken woman. He deserved better. I needed to show him something positive. Give him something he could hold onto when life got hard. I wiped my eyes and cleared my throat before pressing record again and sitting back down on the cushion beside Oscar. I couldn't look at him if I wanted to get the words out without crumbling. Instead I picked him up, cuddling him close to my chest, focusing once again on the lifeless lens of the camera.

"Darling. Oscar... Being your mother has been the best time of my life, and I love you more than you can ever know. I'm sorry that I won't always be here with you, so I need to tell you this now. Whoever you become, whatever you do, I will always love you. I support you to the ends of the earth, I hope you will be able to feel that, even when I'm gone. You are going to have big decisions to make in your life, there will be difficult times where you might not know which path to take. Times when you need me there to guide you, love you, support you. I'm sorry I can't do that, my angel, if I could, believe me, I would do anything to change it. There is nothing I wouldn't do if it meant I could stay with you. Nothing."

"But in the almost eight months since you arrived on this earth, I have seen who you are, and I already know you are strong, you are so sweet, you are filled with kindness and love and curiosity and joy. You are a good person and I know that will never change. Even when you make a bad choice, even when you do something you regret, it won't change who you are fundamentally. Whenever you find yourself in a challenging situation, look inside. Let your heart guide you."

"And though I won't be here, you won't be alone. Not ever. You have the most wonderful father who will love you hard enough for the both of us. Your

Auntie Isabel will always be there for you. Auntie Bonnie too," I added, hoping it would be true. I kissed Oscar's head again and realised he had drifted off to sleep against me as I'd been talking.

"I know you'll wonder where I am, darling. You won't be able to see me again. But though my body will be gone, my energy, the essence that fills me, and all of us, will continue on. I will become the trees, the flowers, even the wind. Energy never dies, sweetheart. It just changes form. Maybe, if you stay very still and think of me, you'll be able to feel all the love I have for you. I hope so."

I looked up to see Lucas standing in the doorway, watching me silently, tears streaming down his cheeks and suddenly I couldn't hold back my grief a second longer. I felt my composure shatter as the reality of what I had just done hit me hard in the chest, my throat closing up, tears pouring from my red, irritated eyes.

"Take us home," I sobbed, reaching out a hand to Lucas. "Please, take us home now."

Chapter Twenty-Five

The car pulled into our driveway after a long, quiet journey home and I gasped, reaching for Lucas's hand and squeezing tightly. "Bonnie," I whispered. "It's Bonnie." She was sitting on the doorstep, her arms wrapped tightly around her body, and even from my position in the passenger seat I could tell she'd changed considerably in the year since I'd last laid eyes on her. She stood, approaching the car tentatively, and I felt Lucas squeeze my hand hard as he drew in a deep breath. There were dark circles beneath her eyes, contrasting painfully with her lily white complexion. Her lips were rosy red, swollen and chapped, and her cheeks were sunken, giving her the appearance of some sort of ghostly clown. Her frame had always been slender, but now it was almost skeletal. My Bonnie. My sweet little Bonnie. I stepped out of the car, my legs shaking, and she smiled widely, a shadow of the girl I knew lingering on in her expression.

"Hey Sis," she said, her voice soft, husky.

I grabbed her by the collar of her jacket, pulling her into me with such force I thought I might break her. She was here. Really here. "I missed you so much you bloody fool. Where have you been?"

Lucas stepped out of the car, walking slowly around to us, saving Bonnie from having to answer. Bonnie pulled back from me, smiling at Lucas. "Hey Bro."

He dipped his head, leaning in to kiss her on the cheek. "Welcome back."

"Thanks." She shuffled her feet, concealing a shiver and I realised she was freezing. "So, can I meet him?" Bonnie asked, nodding towards the car.

"Oscar?"

She nodded.

"Of course you can," I laughed. "Of course you can!"

Thirty minutes later, after Bonnie had finally got to hold her nephew for the first time, Lucas took him out for a walk in the pram leaving Bonnie and I to talk. Having waited so long I found I didn't know where to begin. How to ask what had been happening with her. How to even start to explain what *I'd* been going through. I was scared anything I told her would push her right over the edge, and Bonnie seemed to sense this. She came to sit beside me on the sofa, taking my hand between hers. I flinched at how cold they were, the feel of her bones and tendons flexing beneath the paper thin surface. "It's not as bad as it seems," she smiled, looking into my eyes. "I'm actually on the mend – no really," she insisted as I raised an eyebrow in disbelief. "It's not been the easiest year, and I've made some stupid decisions, but things are getting better. I promise, Roxy."

I shook my head, not sure how to respond. I didn't believe her, but she seemed so level headed, so sure. "Bonnie, I... I have to tell you something."

Bonnie dipped her face and when she looked back up I saw that she was crying. "I know. I got back a few days ago. Rox, you don't have to say anything. Isabel already did."

"She told you? That I'm... That I'm going to –"

"She told me everything. She didn't want to, but I know when she's keeping a secret. Twin thing," she shrugged. "Roxy, I'm sorry I was too selfish to be here for you when you needed me."

"Don't say that! You aren't selfish. You couldn't have stayed, not when you had so much you needed to work through yourself. I understand that. I do."

"I've wasted so much time with you. I should have been here."

"You're here now."

She put her arms around me, her forehead resting on mine. "Tell me what you need from me, please. There must be something I can do."

I sighed. "I need you to tell me the truth. I need to know what's going on with you. I need you to be well and whole and happy again..."

"I'm trying." She leaned back against the cushions, rubbing her eyes. "It wasn't your fault. You have to know that. I was already struggling... for a really long time. The accident just triggered something in me and I couldn't come back from that."

"What is it, sweetheart? What happened?"

"I think you know. I think I knew too, but I couldn't face it. I didn't want it to be true. I didn't want to end up like..."

"Like mum?" I murmured. "Bon, is it... do you

have Bipolar?" She looked at me, her eyes on mine for a very long time, unable to speak. Finally, she gave a nod.

"I tried to fight it, but I wasn't strong enough. I didn't know what to do, how to keep going, how to be normal. I didn't want to hurt you, like she did."

"Oh, Bonnie." I took her hand. "You know, I never blamed mum for what happened. Not really."

"I did. I hated her for leaving me."

"You know she wouldn't have if she had been well. You know she loved us."

"I do now... at least, I'm starting to."

"Bonnie... is me, uh, leaving," I said, unwilling to use the word dying. "Is it going to throw things off balance for you again? I couldn't bear the thought of you struggling because of me."

"So stay."

"You know I can't."

"I do... Isabel explained." She shook her head. "I'm seeing a doctor. I'm on meds. And I have time, I guess, time to prepare for losing... for losing..." Her words faded away and she wrapped her arms tightly around me, sobbing into my shoulder. "I wish I could change it. It's not fair."

"Me too," I whispered back. "But promise me, you'll stay well. You'll take the meds. You won't let losing me destroy you. Promise me, Bon, you have to promise me!"

"I promise," she replied.

A few hours later I climbed into bed having fed Oscar, watching in pleasure as his eyes had grown heavy, his breathing becoming deeper as he surrendered to sleep. His breath was sweet and milky as I kissed him softly, wishing him sweet dreams and placing him down on the mattress. Lucas got into bed on the other side of me and I turned to face him. "So is she going to be okay?" he asked, moving a strand of hair behind my ear.

"I hope so. Will you look after her?"

"You know I will."

"I do."

I rested my head on his chest, listening to the strong, reassuring sound of his heart. I felt a peace that had been out of reach for so long now. Seeing Bonnie had been something I had longed for since the moment she'd left. She was going to be okay. They all were. There were people who would love Oscar when I couldn't do it. Lucas would continue to be kind and strong and utterly gorgeous, and though it hurt to think of it, I knew he would find someone to love, someone to be happy with again. My family would grieve. They would mourn and they would eventually move on with their lives, thinking of me often.

"I love you, Roxy," Lucas said, his breath on my hair.

"I love you too." He kissed me, his mouth soft, the perfect fit against my own. Then I closed my eyes, holding onto him tightly. My hand reached out behind me to hold Oscar's soft little fingers, and I felt a tear slip from the corner of my eye.

A few hours later I woke, unmoving, feeling the slow rise and fall of Lucas's chest beneath my cheek, the butterfly light touch of my son's hand in my own. The room was dark and still. The pain came fast, sudden but not entirely unexpected, and then there was nothing. It was over.

Lucas

Three years later.

If someone had asked me back then if I thought I could heal from losing you, I would have laughed in their face. I didn't believe you would actually go. I never accepted it as a possibility, not really. When we sprinkled your ashes over the South Downs, Bonnie half drunk and already on a path of self destruction despite her best efforts, I thought we would all crumble and die. The sheer cliff edge was perhaps a poor choice for a group as unstable as we were back then. I didn't see any way to move forward, any way to help your sisters, our son through the devastation of losing you. I wanted to die too. I wanted to be the one who got to leave if one of us had to. How cruel that I had to stay to pick up the pieces when all I could think of was joining you. I don't believe in Hell, at least not for the dead, but after that first year without you I know it exists for the living. I was there.

But you left me with something to ease the pain. You left me with a purpose, my salvation. Oscar. If it wasn't for him, I don't know how I would have survived losing you. But the thing about babies is, they don't care if you're grieving. They don't care if you can't face getting out of bed. They're in the moment, right here, right now. If something's funny, they laugh, even if it's not appropriate. If they're hungry, you need to get up and feed them. You just have to.

Oscar taught me a lot about grieving. He didn't hold back. His longing for you was unbearable those first few months. He cried constantly. He was angry and lost and it broke my heart because there was nothing I could do to fix it for him. He needed you. But then, I guess time healed his pain.

I waited. I was there to hold him through both of our tears. And at some point, he began to smile again. He accepted his new world. He let you go. Eventually, I learned to do the same. Not because we stopped loving you, but because, in time, things became more bearable. We were busy. He was growing and changing day by day. You not being here became our normal. And though we talk of you often, and Oscar asks how you would have felt about his painting, his new toy, our trip to the beach and everything else, we've learned to keep going without you somehow.

The first time I realised I was happy, I felt overcome with guilt. How could I feel happiness ever again? How could I leave you behind and move on with my life? But as time has passed, we've smiled more. We've laughed. We have found a new reality and honestly, we're okay. I know you would want that for us. I know you would want us to be happy.

The wounds that were so raw and open when you left, have healed now. There are deep scars etched on all of us that will never be erased, but they don't hurt so much these days, unless I pull at the edges. I try not to do that too often.

I miss you, Roxy. I miss us. I miss what could have been. What *should* have been. But I'm okay. Really. I'm grateful for the time we had, the memories we made, the son we created. I'm grateful for every minute we had together, even the bad ones, the hard times. It's all part of our story and I tell it to Oscar often. I know how scared you were at the thought of leaving us. I know you thought we would fall apart, and we did. But we put ourselves back together. I want you to know, life is good. We are happy. We'll be okay.

I have written to you so many times since you left, each time lighting a fire in the back garden, sending the words out into the universe as I hold them into the flames. I'm not ready to stop. I don't know if I'll ever be. But I don't feel the need to do it so often now.

Oscar and I are going to the park in a minute. It's hot, the kind of day you loved best, and we're planning to buy ice creams. He'll have something with chocolate, just like you would have done. He loves hearing all the ways you and he are similar. He loves you so very much, sweetheart, and he knows you love him too.

So now, I'll go. I won't say goodbye, you and I have been through too many of those. I'll just say, until the next time. Until I have to tell you something only you would understand. Until I can't resist sharing my secrets with you. I love you, Roxy. And I forgive you for not being here.

Sleep peacefully angel,

Lucas.

About This Story

I was at my annual visit to the hairdressers, waiting for the highlights to take and basking in a child free afternoon when one of the girls walked past and popped a stack of magazines on the table in front of me to flick through. The pile was mostly made up of those real life type mags, the ones filled with true, or at least vaguely true stories, and the kind of which I would usually avoid. I can't stand them. The tales tend to be horror filled and traumatic and due to my over active imagination, they can haunt me for years. To this day, I still have stories I wish I could erase from my mind.

I'm not sure what prompted me to reach for the dog-eared magazine off the top of the pile that afternoon. Perhaps it was a catchy headline, perhaps a picture I couldn't help but learn more about. I don't remember. What I do remember is the piece I read. It was about a mother who gave birth to her first child and got to enjoy him for two idyllic weeks before being diagnosed with breast cancer. The cancer was aggressive and spreading fast and the mother's health quickly deteriorated.

What followed was a year of intensive chemotherapy, abject terror, separation and disruption for their newly formed family. It seemed certain that she wouldn't make it. I believe, in the end this mother did pull through, though the details are fuzzy now after so long. What mattered to me though, what stuck with me long after putting the magazine back on the pile, was the fear she must have felt at the idea of leaving her brand new baby without a mother to raise him.

As a mother to two young children it affected me deeply and got me thinking. What would happen to them if I wasn't around. If I died, would they ever know how much they meant to me, how much I loved them, or would they always wonder? Would they be able to have a decent happy life without me? What about my husband? I had promised him a lifetime together, and checking out early would be a betrayal of the hopes and dreams we shared.

How can a person break the news to the people they love, that they have to say goodbye? How can they stand to shatter their hearts and yet have no way of changing their fate?

Writing has always been a comfort to me, knowing that I'm leaving a part of myself behind for my family to look back on, but One More Tomorrow has gone a step further. It forced me to consider the things I would want my children to know if I weren't here to tell them myself. That I love them beyond all measure. That I accept them unconditionally for who they are now and whoever they become in the future. That I believe in them, I know deep in my heart the goodness, the kindness, the sweetness that shines from them. That no matter what wrong turns they may take, I know they will find their way back.

It has been my way of writing my legacy of love to them. In fact, the title was very nearly going to be Legacy, only I decided it was too much of a spoiler.

As mothers, we see ourselves as the glue, the thing that creates order, fights without restraint for the benefit of our children and as such we can't fathom how they could continue on without us. It is both wonderful and terrifying to play such an important role in another person's life.

What this book has allowed me to see and to understand is that life continues whether we are there to see it or not. People grieve desperately, they remember those they have loved and lost, but somehow, they find a way to adapt, to continue and to smile again.

I hope that anyone facing the fear of leaving someone they love due to disease or illness will find comfort in the pages of this book. Your life, however long or short, has meaning, beauty. Your presence will have made a difference to those who know you. And the people you care about will forge a new path, never forgetting, but moving forward all the same. This has been the greatest comfort to me.

Someone asked me if this story had a happy ending and I didn't know how to answer. No, Roxy didn't survive. No miracle occurred and saved her. Yet I believe the ending, if not happy is one of immense positivity. What I hope it conveys is the importance of living a life filled with love, meaning, real experiences. Of not wasting time. And of knowing that the people we leave behind will be okay in the end.

Life is fleeting, make yours something wonderful.

Lots of love,

Sam

I would love to hear your thoughts so please head over to Amazon to leave a review and let me know if you enjoyed this story. I am grateful for every review I receive.

To be the first to find out about new book releases, giveaways and more, sign up to my newsletter at www.samvickery.com

The Promise

Available on Amazon worldwide

Chapter One

Emily leaned over the tiny stainless steel sink, pulling her long black hair to one side and holding it in place as she bent forward to wash her face. The water splashed down onto the dark haired baby she wore strapped to her chest, and he squealed nuzzling his cheek into her cardigan, rubbing the moisture away. She winced as the icy water turned her fingertips blue, and reached over to the soap dispenser only to find it empty. Again.

Sighing, she took a handful of paper towels and rubbed the rough surface over her skin until she was dry. She took one more and held it under the trickling tap, then squeezed it in her fingers, watching the excess water filter away. She leaned forward, dangling the baby backwards so that she could reach his face, and deftly used the damp paper to clean his skin.

He arched away and she dipped into the woven wrap, locating a sticky hand and pulling it free. She cleaned it thoroughly and then found the other one. "No need to look so worried Flynn," she muttered. "It's way to cold for a big wash, you're getting away with the bare minimum today, lucky boy!"

She tossed the paper towel into the bin and grabbed her backpack, slinging the heavy weight onto her shoulders. Loud, happy voices echoed through the public toilets, and Emily looked behind her to see two women entering, one blonde and soft looking, one pixie like redhead, both pushing buggies overladen with changing bags and souvenirs. Emily immediately spotted a plastic bag with the Natural History Museum logo on it and smiled widely. Jackpot.

Without a doubt, the best thing about being homeless in London was the tourists. They never failed to surprise her with their sheer naivety. Stealing from them, conning them in some way or another, it was almost too simple. But Emily didn't crave challenge, she didn't wish they would make it a little harder to get what she wanted. What she craved was food. Money to buy clothes for her growing son, safety. Day to day life was challenging enough. The easy tourists were a gift and she hoped these two wouldn't let her down.

Emily smiled confidently at them and pushed her numerous fake gold and silver bangles up her forearm, pointing to the two sleeping toddlers in their buggies. "Long day?" she asked.

"Yes," the blonde woman sighed happily. "We've seen everything. They've had so much fun!"

"How old are they?"

"Both two. This is Thomas," she said, pointing to the red cheeked, blonde haired boy in front of her. "And this is Elizabeth," she gestured to her friend's child. "How old is yours?"

Emily looked down at her son, smiling with pride. "He's ten months."

"You're not wearing any shoes," the pixie woman exclaimed, noticing the dirty bare feet poking out from beneath her flowing skirt. "Is this a new fashion thing? You must be freezing!"

"Uh, no, not a fashion thing. More a stepped in a

big puddle thing. They're in my bag. I was just going to go and get some new ones for the journey home," she lied, not wanting to tell them the truth. That she had swapped her shoes last week for a BLT and a Starbucks latte with "Woozy Susie." It had been getting dark and Emily hadn't eaten all day, when Susie, a no nonsense, afro haired, pickled livered, sixty year old woman who had been on the streets most her life, had struck up the deal with her. She had been too hungry to even think of saying no.

For some reason, and she couldn't fathom why, she got a lot less charity than others in the area. You would think that with a baby, people would be falling over themselves to help her, but it wasn't like that. If anything, they judged her harder and ignored her even more than the standard prescription for the misfortunate. If only they knew what she had been through to end up in this situation. If only they would open their minds for a second and give her a chance to explain.

So, she had no shoes. In October. In London. But she did have a pair of thick woollen socks. She just wasn't about to ruin them walking around the streets in the filth and wet all day, when she could save them and have warm, dry feet tonight.

"I see," the red head said uneasily, breaking eye contact. Emily smiled warmly, and looked away. Her goal was to look wholesome and trustworthy, not an easy thing to accomplish when she was waiting for an opportunity to prove them wrong, but she had been around long enough to know how to play the game. Hell, even before her street life she'd had to hone her skills as an actress.

Pretending. Lying. Trying to keep *him* from seeing the truth, to keep herself safe from his volatile mood swings. She shuddered, not surprised by the sudden turn of her thoughts. She regularly had flashbacks and nightmares, and she thought she saw him at least twice a week. She would be walking along the street and there he would be, striding purposefully towards her. Or sitting on the platform at the train station. Eating a sandwich outside a café.

When that happened, she would melt into the walls, hide her face and hold her breath. She couldn't risk him finding her, finding Flynn. It always took her hours to resume her sense of normality after these false sightings.

But right now, she needed to focus. She glanced over at the women. The pixie was taking a tampon out of her bag, the blonde busily peeling back the blanket from the hot, sleeping child. She needed them to feel comfortable, to see her as just another mother, not as a potential threat. She turned on the water again, making a show of washing her hands. Stalling. The two women parked their buggies beside the sinks and both of them went into the stalls.

Unbelievable, Emily thought, shaking her head. Though she had seen it time and time again, she still couldn't understand what must be going through their minds. To leave not only their belongings, their valuables, but also their precious children right there for the taking in a dirty, public toilet in the middle of London. Emily instinctively wrapped her arms around Flynn, sick at the thought of what could happen if the wrong person saw the unattended children.

Perhaps, she thought introspectively, her fear was a product of her past. Maybe these women had led such blessed lives that they couldn't fathom a time when life would strike them down and leave them ruined. She hoped they would never have to face the consequences of such trusting naivety.

She waited three seconds, wiping her palms dry on her skirt, then walked straight to where the two toddlers were sleeping, completely unaware of the world around them. With expert fingers, she slid a handful of nappies, a packet of wet wipes and one of the two purses from the open bags. She riffled through the purse and found forty pounds in cash.

Grinning, she slipped the now empty purse back into the bag and without hesitating a second longer, walked straight out of the toilets. Forty pound! She felt like jumping up and down with excitement. They would be eating tonight. And she might even splash out and buy some shoes if she could find a cheap pair. She made for the back streets, knowing they would never find her, already pushing their faces from her mind.

She never let herself think about the effect her actions would have on the people she targeted. She couldn't. Yes, it was harsh, yes it would be a little crack in their otherwise perfect day, but she never took credit cards or personal things, and she knew they would manage without it. What would be a nice takeaway or a family day out for them, would mean her and Flynn could eat every day for a fortnight or maybe more. She didn't feel bad taking from them. It was necessary.

Emily could feel the eyes burning into her back as she walked the aisles of the busy supermarket, a basket slung over her arm. She had found a pair of trainers only one size too big for four pounds in the sale bin, and she had made straight for the reduced food section, marked down because it only had a few hours of shelf life left. Four sandwiches marked at thirty pence each and a tub of strawberries for ten pence lay alongside the shoes in her basket. She glanced over her shoulder to see the young, burly security guard following closely behind. This was bullshit. She had money in her pocket and she knew she hadn't done anything wrong.

Emily hated the way people treated her because she was struggling. Homeless. They were scared of her, wary, and she couldn't stand it. This time two years ago she had been shopping in Waitrose, driving a Fiat, a part of society. She had lost everything in the course of one day, but that didn't change who she was deep down. It wasn't fair.

And though she didn't bat an eye at stealing one on one, she would never take the risk of stealing from a real shop. She wouldn't dare, for fear of being hemmed in by security. Of not being able to get out. Of having them take Flynn from her. She was always on her best behaviour in places like this. So why on earth was he following her?

"Miss?"

She turned, a false smile plastered on her face. "Yes?"

"I'm going to have to ask you to leave, if you could just follow me please," the guard said, reaching forward and forcibly taking her basket from her.

"What? Why?"

"You know your kind aren't allowed in here."

"My kind?" she asked, reeling from his insult.

"You know."

"No, I don't. I haven't a clue what you're on about. I just want to buy my food and I'll be going," she said, reaching to take the basket from him.

"Don't make a scene. Come on, let's go."

"No! What have I done? I'm trying to buy food for my son, I haven't done anything wrong!"

"We have enough of you lot coming in here and taking stuff without paying. This ain't a charity love. Go to a soup kitchen or somethin', but don't be coming back here. You ain't welcome."

"I'm not homeless, I'm a backpacker. Fuck. I didn't do anything wrong, just let me buy the food."

"You ain't got no money, look at you, you don't even have any shoes on and the kids not dressed for this weather," he said, pointing at Flynn's bare feet.

"I'm buying shoes, look!" she shouted, pointing at the basket. "How am I supposed to wear shoes if you won't let me buy them?"

A crowd of curious onlookers was beginning to form at the end of the aisle, though Emily noticed that they kept a safe distance away. Wouldn't want to get too close to the crazy homeless lady now, would they? The guard glanced at them, frowning, then leaned towards Emily, a menacing expression on his face.

"Do I need to call for assistance or are you gonna

get out?"

Emily glared at him venomously, hatred burning in her eyes. It wasn't fair. None of this was fair. Every ounce of her wanted to fight this, to stand up for herself and win. But she couldn't risk it. The police would never take her side, that was just the way it went. With an angry grunt, she let go of the basket, her gaze resting briefly on the food she wouldn't get to eat. The shoes she wouldn't get to wear. "Fine. I'll go somewhere else," she said, her fist clenching tightly around the money in her pocket.

With all the dignity she could muster, she turned and walked away, the sound of the crowd's disapproving mutters ringing in her ears. His heavy footsteps followed behind her all the way to the exit.

The Promise is available now on Amazon worldwide.